THE REASON I'M HERE

THE REASON I'M HERE

First paperback edition published by Stalking Horse Press, June 2023

Library of Congress Control Number: 2023936986

A version of "1 John 3:15" was published in Issue #4 of *The Kraken's Spire*
A version of "Useless, Useless" published by Roi Fainéant Press

Publishing Editor: James Reich
Design by James Reich

Stalking Horse Press
Santa Fe, New Mexico

www.stalkinghorsepress.com

M.R.,
THANK YOU for hosting such an amazing
event. Your words, space, and time are
so very appreciated.

JARROD CAMPBELL

THE REASON
I'M HERE

STALKING HORSE PRESS
SANTA FE, NEW MEXICO

CONTENTS

*For Christian Stewart Barnett
and Diana Lynn Campbell*

The great art of life is sensation, to feel that we exist, even in pain...
—Lord Byron

THERE'S A REASON I'M HERE

If April showers bring May flowers, then what do May flowers bring? Pilgrims!

THE TERRIBLE dry joke David's grandfather told him many years ago flashes through his thoughts as his feet pound wet pavement. His laughter keeps him from registering the danger until it's too late. Glimpsing final patches of green and small flowers just beyond the concrete curb, rounding the bend in the road, David loses his footing. Everything turns black—

Slowly, the black becomes neutral. Gray rain drizzles and soaks his clothes. How long has he been laying in the street? Why is he laying in the street? Pain cracks his skull when he sits upright. Pressure begins from the back and wraps around both sides of his head to meet in the middle, cleaving a perfect bisection between his eyes. David doesn't want to lie down again. His body does not seem to belong to him. Leg muscles lift him vertical, off the pavement, and to an undisclosed location; a miracle since there is nothing he can remember. *Where are his feet taking him? More importantly, who is he?*

The key in his pocket fits, thank God. And how grateful for the muscle memory of his legs, or whatever served as an internal homing device.

"You're back early. Too wet?"

David flinches when the man approaches for a kiss.

"You okay?" the man asks, before adding, "You forgot to take off your shoes."

"I think I also forgot a few other things," David says, just above a whisper, before he collapses to the floor.

. . .

My name is David Flanigan. I am thirty-nine years old.
My husband's name is Ian Flanigan.

These are the only truths he knows, and only because the man—his husband Ian—has told him so many times. All of it has to be true. Acceptance insists. Endless repetitions of past facts become new memories. Rediscovered skills or passions are successful ways to occupy available time. A particular love of reading is a blessing, but his reactions when rereading what Ian says were his favorite books are shocking for their constant dismissal: "not really good at all." Camus becomes unbearable. *The Stranger*, his true favorite book, is now a chore at a mere one hundred and twenty-three pages. But Jane Austen becomes an obsession. This is the first real sign of David becoming someone else.

The books are only the beginning of a melancholy that threatens to outlast him. Every crack in his memory breaks his heart. It's as bad for Ian, poor man, who now also has to offer up his life all over again. He'll gladly do so for the sake of the man he loves. Six years together to scrutinize and reevaluate. Only the better part of those six years will survive. That's a decision Ian makes very early.

. . .

"There's a reason I'm here," David states one morning in their kitchen, standing by the refrigerator.

"Milk for your coffee?" Ian suggests. He assumes David has had another short-term memory lapse.

"No, not that. I mean why I'm here, on this earth." This thought lodges itself in David's head and begins to demand, in secret, more consideration.

. . .

David stares at the row of six giant lightbulbs that line the bathroom mirror. Each time he blinks, it lasts several seconds, enough time to become temporarily blind, whether his eyes are open or closed. The windowless bathroom is too bright. A quick finger flips the light switch and plunges him into darkness. Even in the dark with his eyes closed tight, the memory of wire filaments transmutes into two crescent moons that shine side-by-side like an ominous astrological occurrence. No eyesight for a few seconds, then a dazzling radiance illuminates his head, surrounded by the complete darkness of the bathroom. This comes to mean more than the rest of these new days and their exasperating hours where shadows and obscurity choke out his yearning for real enlightenment.

. . .

Friends.
Their friends.

They start coming around more often to give David new memories he regrets forgetting. "That sounded fun!" is genuine the first time, but each flashback tied to a slew of photos on someone's cellphone begins to wear him down. A new cellphone for David replaces the one broken or lost during the accident and has nothing important to show. All attempts to reintroduce social media fail. True, these are David's memories, his thoughts, or reactions, but not anymore. That part of his life is unrecognizable, just like so much else. Ian is a master at reading David's body language, not the veneer that sugar coats his words. People understand. They're friends, after all. Their friends. Friends. Ian's friends. David doesn't appear to have friends apart from those shared with his husband, none of his own. Perfect, he thinks. Less obligation to other people and more time to focus on Ian, his beautiful guide and fellow traveler through the past six years of their life.

. . .

Uncovering a lover's body for the first time is enthralling given the integers making up the sum. Learning all over how to make love to somebody, even a second chance at a first time, is nerve wracking. There is a novelty to everything, the feel of another man's body against him, inside him, on top of him, the choreography of sex, the investments made to accommodate the physical love of another man. A natural, synonymous motion is achieved with little effort. The procedures reactivate old motors that Ian finds pleasurable, much to David's satisfaction. All in all, efficient and effervescent flesh-covered machines, in the end. David learns how much he enjoys the physicality of his relationship with Ian. So much has been difficult to undertake, let alone believe, but the sex is a welcome reward for all the minor trifles and headaches of settling back into a life. If there is a way to remember with whom—in the past—he's shared his body, sweat, saliva, and tears, David hopes to find out how. Asking might be in poor taste.

. . .

Mountains of papers exist for David to sign at the legal office of Jonathan E. D. Roman, Esquire. Ian insists it's a good idea that he have full power of attorney for the first year after the accident. All the explanations make sense to David, so without any reluctance, he consents. *What do I know about any of this, anyway?* David wonders. He is startled when his hand automatically produces a quality signature that he scrawls on so many dotted lines. Now he's completely dependent on Ian. When he thinks about that reality, David tells himself it's for the best, and this is repeated in his ear as each paper becomes an official document.

Already so reliant on Ian, David further resigns himself to feeling cumbersome and indebted. The appointment with Roman opens David's eyes to the small fortune he has spread across several bank accounts. The good conscience that facilitates gratitude wants David to tell Ian that he can take however much money, whenever he wants. There's no price he can repay for the kindness he has been shown. So, he does. Ian shows his appreciation by smiling and kissing David's hand. But he declines, even though on paper and now by permission, he has every right.

"This is only for a year, while you recover," Ian says before he reassures. "You'll be back to your old self soon enough... less than a year, I'll bet."

The only thing constant in life is change. David remembers reading that recently, somewhere. David likes who he is, minus the amnesia. That will be cured, or overcome, or whatever the victory is called. A tiny voice, too small and easy to miss, whispers something so ridiculous that David wouldn't believe it anyway. And yet, the seed is planted.

What if I don't want to become the old me again?

Once the paperwork is final, the lawyer requests to see Ian in private.

"It's okay, I can do it with him here. It won't take long." Ian's words are swift, unsure, unsteady, just like his hands as he accepts the thin manila envelope from the confused, concerned lawyer. But Ian's motions as he rips the envelope first in half, then once again in quarters, show no hesitation, only composure.

"What did you rip up?" David asks on the way home.

"Nothing important. If it was for you, then you would've seen it and signed it."

The explanation is sufficient for David. It's easier to forget about insignificant details with the belief that doing so frees up room for more imperative things to have a place to stay when they come back. There's opportunity for more pressing ideas and new recollections to germinate and grow.

. . .

Rain makes David morose. Gray skies run parallel with dull streets and sidewalks, and a sudden chill halts the approach of warmer climate. A rainy day had changed his life forever. He refuses to leave the house when it's wet outside, the fear of another slip and fall too paralyzing. For a few days after waking up from his coma, he is convinced that another blow to his head could possibly reset the damage from the first. So, he asks his doctor, who tells him just how horrible an idea that is. Now he wonders if anything will break through the fog inside his mind. Doubts skulk about, more brazen the longer they're left unchecked.

. . .

Sunny days bring better spirits, but a resilient, lingering chill dampens David's hopes for absolute fulfillment, for safety, and the return of his confidence. There's an atypical air to Ian's speech, movement, and manner. The cooler temperature outside isn't that bad, he insists. David is jealous of Ian's blossoming optimism and in secret hopes it's contagious. "Just keep in mind that warmer weather is right around the corner," Ian suggests. David smiles with the covert hope that his own improvement will follow the season's lead and awaken, revived. Memories should imitate the dormant buds popping open on trees and from the still cold earth.

David and Ian share the popular opinion that nicer weather is here to stay. The restaurants are packed whenever they go out to eat or drink with friends. Their friends. "Well, Ian thinks so more than I do," David awkwardly insists. Instead of the lighthearted jab he intends to make, the opinion makes others think he's only along out of duty. Only a few people hear the remark over dinner and cocktails, but his reputation as an unwilling guest is born from texts and chats between all the friends. In a week's time, they'll all be Ian's friends only. No longer their friends. When enough people say and believe something, that's enough to cement it in a tomb of truth.

"It's okay if you don't want to come along," Ian says, the next time.

"I don't understand," David begins, defeated and ignoring what Ian just said. "Was it something I said? Did I do something wrong? Should I have been picking up the check every time?"

"Who can say?" Ian offers with an unconvincing tenor just below the surface of his words. "Maybe they just aren't used to the new David yet, because they really loved the old David."

"Which one do you love more? David asks.

"I love you, David."

Kisses and flesh hit their marks with requisite exhilaration. Within minutes the job is done, and both men end pleased with the resulting sweat and smiles. Too satisfied to care what anybody else thinks, David tells Ian to go on without him and also to offer up any excuse that sounds sensitive, yet believable. Ian smiles in agreement.

"You know," Ian starts, halfway out the open front door, "I think I may appreciate the new David just a little more."

A kiss sent down the hallway on an exhaled rush of air never makes it to the intended target because there is nothing really there at all. How easy to play along and go through the compulsory motions of a six-year-old love affair.

. . .

Freedom is given alongside an increase in trust. Improvement is impressive, all the doctors say so. Motor skills and cognitive functions continue to progress better than anybody expected. The past leading up to his fall is still elusive and the main cause of concern, to nobody more than David himself. But that doesn't impact the aptitude to drive or navigate destinations with a GPS showing the way. With relative quickness, David is driving himself between appointments and taking the car out for no reason other than to get out of the house. The need for fresh air becomes paramount to his sanity. With Ian back to work, but from his home office, he's either alone at the desk David's not allowed near, or next to David like an attentive pup.

"Oh, hi Jonathan," David says. "Ian didn't mention any meetings today. What did we forget to sign?"

A mind more tuned in to the setting and condition of the people involved might read the skittish physicality between Ian and Jonathan as the result of inappropriate behavior. The initial closeness diminishes in degrees. There is something off-putting in the way Ian physically interrupts Jonathan, stepping between the beginning sentence and David. "He's just leaving," Ian sputters.

Jonathan offers an obvious impromptu of words, "I can come by again when I get the papers drawn up." He bumps into Ian brusquely as he walks past to leave. Barely a nod is offered to David.

"What papers?" David inquires.

"I was going to have my will changed a bit."

A convinced David drops the subject. Ian says to his husband: "You can be here when Jonathan brings them by the next time, right Jonathan?"

Those words echo down the hall and add fury to the force already responsible for a vigorous slamming of the front door. Ian breezes unbothered through the intuitive motions: the customary hug and kiss when coming home, the back and forth about what happened during their time apart. A brief flashback from when David found Jonathan and Ian close together interjects itself into a smile meant to reaffirm that a new David is alive inside the old skin and bones of his former self. Ian reciprocates, but then flinches at how David physically interrupts him from speaking by stepping in and giving him another, much deeper kiss.

"So, what's for lunch? I'm starving?"

. . .

A sheen of sweat covers their bodies, the sheets suffering the worst from dampness. The intimacy of two people is sublime, their arms and legs locked in an attempt to fuse more of themselves together as a singular entity. David is grateful for the gift of the present tense, of being in the moment, especially during sex. Burgeoning appreciation is shown by being open to anything Ian desires. After the act, when the need for mindfulness relaxes, frustration creates the urge to know, which prompts him to ask, "What is your favorite memory with me from the past six years?"

"I'd say the memories we're making now matter more."

"That's sweet," David says genuinely and follows with a kiss. "But what about in the past? Something I can't remember."

"The past is the past, what does it matter?"

"It matters because I can't remember any of it."

"Would you believe me if I told you, anyway?"

An off-hand comment like that once made David angry enough to shout and search for any item within arm's reach to break or tear in half. The past Ian knows appears spotted with these blemishes.

"I believe everything you tell me. I don't really have much of a choice."

"You can always believe me. I have no reason to lie."

This sentence and a caress soothe the leery look that had wrinkled David's brow.

"I have a lot of favorite memories. Trips we've taken, people we've known, things like that. But honestly, my favorite memory is how and why we met."

David's eyes light up at the prospect of hearing this story again. No detail is easier to recount than the instant their story began. A nondescript coffee chain, the one found on every corner. Ian was before David in line, the hypnotic shifting of his hips while standing there kept David staring. He delighted to learn that Ian's drink was the same as his: a medium whole milk latte. But was this enough to ask him out? Two coincidences only. The best signs always come in threes. A shared taste in pastries became the third sign when Ian ordered. The ensuing conversation served as the clincher. As it was the last pastry, a frosted cinnamon walnut scone, it ended with numbers exchanged and plans to meet at the same coffee shop after work. Ian refused to let David leave without the scone. David was happy to get two things he wanted that morning. The third thing he wanted came later that night; again, always in threes.

A weak smile from David meets the satisfied glee beaming from Ian's face. His overcast stare clouds and dims the room.

"It was the pumpkin scone that we both wanted that day, I thought, because we met in October, just before your birthday at the end of the month. I mean, that's what you told me before."

"Shit, you're right. I was thinking about the pastry we always fight about now."

"And you left out that detail also." Ian's gaze lowers while David continues. "Didn't I sigh out loud, or grumble or something, which is what made you turn around and notice me? You said I was actually pissed you got the last scone, which is why you ended up giving it to me."

Ian nods during David's fretful reporting of the memory. "I know, I know. I left out the bad part on purpose. Sorry." The polite thing to do is wait for David's response. When the delivery never comes, Ian continues. "You're lucky, in a way. There are a lot of things I wish I could forget. But no matter how hard I try to, or try to right the wrong, to show how sorry I am and that I've repented, it still doesn't make some things easy to forget."

"You can tell me tomorrow what some of the bad things from the past are that I can't remember."

"I'd rather just tell you how much I've come to love you since then. And how now I have something, someone else to think about other than myself."

"I didn't give you that before?"

"Well…yes, of course you did."

A head shakes in reluctant acceptance while David repositions his body from upright to horizontal, his head finding rest on Ian's thigh. Still sitting up, Ian strokes David's hair, unsure of whether to speak or not to speak. If he did, what would he have to say? David falls asleep, himself unsure now of so much.

. . .

There's a reason I'm here, David believes. Maybe his losing the past was deliberate, to clear the slate in preparation for something that hasn't happened yet.

. . .

An obvious dream. The house is "theirs" but not where they live. The foreign design and layout of space is navigated with innate ease. The serene and verdant backyard just beyond the patio completes the illusion as further proof of dreaming.

David's thirst, satisfied by a cold glass of water, remains internal but shifts focus and purpose. The house and hall are cool in the early morning, a chill from his heels to the hair on his head makes him shiver while returning to the bedroom. He is naked and so is Ian, half-asleep and sprawled belly-up on the bed. Ian, awake enough to be half propped up under a pillow and fully aroused, absentmindedly fondles his erection. Thirst becomes hunger becomes passion. A desire arises in David to be filled with any mystery Ian proposes, anything he sees fit to give. Whatever Ian offers will never be enough.

Something more waits behind a weakening dam that begs to break from the incredible pressure. The hesitation Ian demonstrates while making love is proof. *What if force comes at it from the other side?* David wonders as he straddles his husband. The rocking back and forth on Ian's lap gains intensity with each landing. Ian pushes back and grabs David's hips to match the aggression directed downward into his own hips and thighs.

Ian sits upright, his back against the clunky headboard

and its rhythmic knocking against the wall. Face to face, eye to eye. Words David hopes will open more of Ian are pacified by the actions of an intrusive tongue. The words get jumbled, not forgotten. David complies. *What if force comes at it from the other side?* he deliberates once again. A pause in the kiss gives David his chance. An unrealized strength from David's open palms breaks Ian's ninety-degree angle when their full force strikes his chest. A sturdy wall allows only so much give, just like the delicacy of a skull. A veritable crack emits from the connection of bone and plaster. With any luck the egg will be open, ready to nourish.

"Whoever you are, this is great," Ian coos, unaware of who is grinding into his lap.

David smiles. The slow realization that no flash of recognition lights Ian's eyes eventually stops David's movement. "Funny," is all David can muster to say.

"I'm not done, but it's cool if you are. You mind if I just jack off, then? I'm really close. Plus, my husband will be home soon, and I really want to get off. You'll have to be long gone before he gets back."

The coldness and facility of Ian's delivery keeps its icy fingers on David's flesh as he shudders awake.

· · ·

"A letter from the law offices of Jonathan E. D. Roman for you, Ian," David says, entering the office to find Ian at his desk. The letter is passed off by hand.

"Wonder what this is," Ian remarks with an anxious inquisitiveness and opens it, examining the single page with care. "What the hell is this?" he asks "Why is he charging me for this?"

"Charging you for what?" David asks in turn.

"For the three weeks you were in a coma. You wouldn't remember that, but he told me he wasn't going to charge me for his counseling during that time."

David has no recollection of being unconscious but does remember Ian telling him that his coma lasted only one week. Did the doctors tell him he was out for three weeks or one? Skepticism creeps in to choke growing self-assurance with ivy-like vines as Ian hastily files the bill away in the bottom desk drawer. David holds fast to what he believes to be true: Ian has lied again.

"Why would he need to counsel you for three weeks?"

"There was so much uncertainty while you were in the hospital…"

There's so much uncertainty now… David thinks.

"Jonathan was helping me understand options, depending on whatever happened."

David continues internalizing his replies. *When I had no option but to lay there, for two weeks more than I originally thought?*

Minimizing the bubbling cynicism before speaking, David asks, "Are you happy with your present option?" His weak smile is obscured and missed thanks to his downward gaze.

"So happy."

"Then tell me some stuff."

"What stuff? I don't want to talk about—what did you call them?—'the bad things from the past that you can't remember,' please."

"That's not what I want to know, right now." Gnawing doubt

eats him from the inside and threatens to claw through his skin, revealing and obscene. *Which is better,* David questions, *doubting what I think I remember, or doubting him, the only person who knows me better than I know myself? Disregard these options and acknowledge the intuition conspiring to create this desire to know.* David blurts out, "Would you ever lie to me about the things I don't remember?"

The question is designed so that Ian's answers will reveal more about himself than he wants. The thread of a fabrication starts to unravel, and the seams are doomed. The proper length of a pause after a question and before its response is exceeded. How telling, David thinks. Fire starts as an ember before igniting in full and spreading outward to warm then burn even the furthest of his extremities. Tense muscles create a subtle tremble. A fuselage of words burns in David's mouth, too near the point of ignition from the heat radiating in his gut. Before their report, the blaze is extinguished and so are the lights.

. . .

The best way to see out is by looking slightly down at an angle instead of trying to look straight out. It still doesn't offer the greatest view, but just enough can be made out with a squinting focus. Exterior light also factors into how clear any action can be viewed. Everything comes head-on, but nothing can see inside. What seems like hours pass before a single shape approaches close enough to peer inward and upward. Countless silhouettes float or scuttle back and forth since there is never enough time to invest so much in one person. This gives closed eyes an eagerness to open and observe the outlines in full, not through slats like semi-closed Venetian blinds. Will the person be friend or foe? This concern is pulled out of unconsciousness along with David. Murky sight clears to reveal Ian, soon in sharp focus.

. . .

There's no memory of what caused the blackout. Countless questions from his doctor never conjure answers. "What's the last thing you remember?" he asks in earnest. Being at home and talking is the general recollection. No specifics.

Other than having no recollection of the hours leading up to it all, no real damage seems to have occurred to David's brain. The physician's quizzical report states that David passed out mid-sentence whiles standing up, not sure what to say in the end. When the doctor asks in private, Ian says what David confirms. They were at home, talking. Standing up suddenly, David fell forward, unconscious. The doctor makes a remark, something about that being good to know. The question David asked doesn't get reported. That's a personal detail, Ian surmises, failing to see any connection between cause and effect.

. . .

With so many holes to fill in, it's no wonder David asks endless questions. Dutiful responses offer furtive tests so Ian lies to test the depths of his husband's faltered retention. The response to the amount of time spent in the hospital during his first coma is a lie of only a week. Nothing, not even a bead of sweat or subtle flinch, offers an indication of nerves or compunction.

David nods acceptance and punctuates the new memory with a kiss then a subtle invitation to bed.

The next day, Ian goes to the desk in his office where secrets hide in plain sight to find the bill from Jonathan Roman, Esquire. He rips it to shreds, then casually tosses the remnants into a trash bag, taking it to the dumpster moments later.

...

Walking on eggshells around David becomes impossible, much to Ian's chagrin. Comfortable, old patterns are ruts in a road forever keeping the wheels locked in place. Catching him in another lie becomes inevitable and David launches into a verbal attack, only to be stopped short, mid-syllable, by a glazed expression and a collapse.

Consciousness comes back before the ambulance even arrives. Vitals checked on the way to the hospital show nothing alarming, other than an elevated heart rate. Understandable, the EMT states, considering. Even the doctor agrees but is more concerned with the possibility of another concussion. David is lucky, no trauma to the brain according to the battery of scans and cognitive tests. He just can't remember what happened leading up to the spell. There's also the fact that he can't recall much of his past before the initial accident, but all cautiously agree that everything forgotten from that time will return. Above all, David considers going home that same day the real stroke of good fortune.

The inevitable question from the doctor comes right before they leave. Ian again mentions a discussion and how quick David stood up before tumbling. When asked if he cares to divulge what they were talking about, Ian declines. "I can tell you that we were arguing." That is all he offers before asking if the doctor has any further questions. "It's been a rough day. I've had to deal with more than I wanted to today and really just want to go home."

"What about David?" the doctor asks because it seems Ian has forgotten.

"I won't forget him."

"Then I won't keep you," the doctor responds after a brief pause.

"Or David," Ian reminds. The tardiness of his concern goes unappreciated by the already retreating doctor.

. . .

"Why don't I have any friends?" David asks.

"You have plenty of friends," Ian responds, then starts naming people that are in fact more Ian's friends than his own. This doesn't go unnoticed or unaddressed.

"If I didn't know you, I wouldn't have ever met them. I sure wouldn't want to know them as well as you do."

A shocking honesty injects itself into every thought that crosses David's mind and it affects what he says and how it's delivered. A new development that darkens David's recently compliant demeanor – an honest reaction to what feels like walls shrinking around him while the ceiling also falls down upon the floor.

"I'm going to ask a stupid question, but just to make sure, you're not the only boyfriend I've ever had? Maybe the first husband?"

"First husband, but not first boyfriend, no. Why that question all of a sudden?" He tries to ease David's mounting anxiety with a weak smile not backed by anything genuine. "All I remember is you so it's like you're all I've ever known."

"That's a bad thing?" Ian moves in closer.

"It's just…not fair. Who was I, before you? What were my parents like? Who were my friends fifteen, twenty years ago? And before you answer, stop. I don't want to know your take on it. I'm not comfortable anymore with secondhand accounts of the life I had before I met you. I expect a biased version of our past six years together. That makes sense. But I have nothing of my own anymore."

"You have me," Ian reiterates, "and I have no reason to lie to you. You have to believe that, at least."

"I think I do."

Offended, Ian slides back a few inches away from David. "You can trust me, David. I love you. Do you love me?"

The pause pushes Ian further away. Three words finish the rejection.

"I don't know."

. . .

With sex, David can forget about anything outside the bedroom. His husband is thrilled at first, but whatever it is that once made sex compulsive quickly fails at its one job. They reach an agreement of twice a week and for David, these two days are all he looks forward to when it becomes more than just a way to release tension. He sloughs off the shackling thoughts that become worries and allows himself to fantasize about fucking whoever he wants. There's no reference, physical attributes get made up on the spot. Ian becomes an ex-lover, a composite of whoever David thinks he should be.

These fancies lose potency for David. No matter who he imagines having sex with, the delivery is still Ian's, and always uniform. One of the best parts about intimate contact is staring into the eyes of a lover, but those eyes are always on Ian's face, on Ian's head, on top of the shoulders supporting David's heels, and so on, down to the satisfying but monotonous dick. The days of the week can change, just not the number of encounters. Real reasons never surface during conversations where important decisions are made.

. . .

"What's your favorite memory with me from the past six years?" David asks unprompted. The thought pops in his head unexpectedly so in turn he asks it with the same surprising immediacy, as though the question has never before been asked.

"It's how and why we met," Ian begins with practiced, machine-like precision. Specifics about scones can't stop Ian from his flawless, uninterrupted monologue. David grows more delighted by each detail. Accuracy is indefinite, his husband is the only one who must know it all by heart. The conviction of Ian's delivery insists.

"Thanks," David responds when the story ends, "that makes me happy. I couldn't remember anything exactly, just that it was at a coffeeshop."

David blurts out another question that blindsides even himself.

"I can trust you, can't I, Ian?"

"Yes! Why do you ask? I told you before that you can."

"I know. And I want to. But I don't know, I can't one hundred percent."

"Have I given you reason not to?" Ian asks, dangerously testing the waters for just how deep David's memory is.

"I don't know. I honestly can't remember."

David appears as he feels, a scared little boy alone in a dark room, too afraid to stand up and look for a way out.

"Well, you can," Ian says, "you always could, and you'll always be able to."

Something in David's silence suggests that he would no longer know the way out of the room at all, even if someone was to turn on the lights.

. . .

Two lives tied in knots. So many tightly-wound loops exist that even if the thread is severed, each individual strand will still bear the marks left from its former life of attachment. The quandary becomes finding the better option: separate but defective physically by the past or stay fastened to a cord that will never stop tying itself off and choking out purpose. Knowing that they're useless either together or apart weighs heavy on David. He can't say whether the same holds true for Ian.

. . .

Summer heat slowly erodes a once vibrant mind, alive with thought, capable of so much understanding and compassion.

Why the worst crimes go unpunished confounds the suffering victim, never the perpetrator. Only the misery continues. Ian knows the reset button to David's mind and uses it three times. First, David must become angry, which happens often enough whenever he has questions about the past. Anger transforms into a rising steam with no outlet, no top to pop. So, it condensates into a tidal wave of shadows cascading from his head to the ends of his feet. Then David wakes up in bed, groggy like he's slept for days. In the end comes gratitude for Ian, who makes sure he's okay and lets him know everything that happened before he blacked out and forgot.

Without his knowing, David's world gets smaller and more claustrophobic resulting from each spell. The advice of not believing how he remembers things makes sure David doubts information not verified by his husband. Lies become truths that support the reconstruction. Nothing can reverse the damage. No reset button exists for their relationship.

. . .

The balm for soothing abrasions runs out fast, David can't figure out why. Smart enough to know but unsteady in his ability to support suspicions means they stay locked inside until a pressure builds up from within that never finds successful release.

. . .

Answers raise more questions, and the hydra becomes invincible. There is no right because David wouldn't know it from wrong, the only real way up is to go down. He wants to believe his feelings, to trust his gut, but doubt begets further doubts to become its own beast of mythic proportions he'll need to slay. Weight burdens every movement. Sluggish blood oozes through fatigued veins and arteries, to and from a heart withering into a lump of coal. Soon that too will be burned up as fuel by a machine already in collapse.

All representations of themselves are separate but equal and never demonstrative of a life lived in tandem. Photographs of family may as well be of strangers. It pains David to wonder whose version of these memories he's really being told when Ian recounts stories of family and friends. Detachment from his own flesh and blood becomes a terrifying final realization to a mind already addled and concussed. The need for physical connections to his past consumes David more than the hope of living happily ever after. Even more than the momentary blissful escape of sex. David never wanted to forget. The fact that he has makes him long for a genuine memory of his own, remembered by himself alone, so he can finally have one piece of his old life back, humble and tucked away, only for himself.

Since pictures only exist on phones or on hard drives, David wanders into the office with the desk that Ian never wants him near.

"What do you have to hide?" David asked once before.

"Nothing at all. You can go through anything in there anytime you want. I just have stuff in a particular order. I don't want you to mess anything up or misplace something." David surveyed the cluttered piles and before he could retort, Ian continued, "It's an organized mess. So please, if you ever want to see anything here, let me know and we'll sit together when I show it to you. But it's really just boring old papers and bills and stuff like that. Not much of it interests me, honestly."

Going through the first drawer, the shallowest of the three, David realizes that Ian is right. Pens, empty notebooks, unopened packs of gum, all are haphazardly strewn throughout the drawer, pretty boring indeed. The second drawer contains a few larger notebooks, all half used and neglected, and a stack of empty manilla folders, mimicking the same mess of the first. Way in the back, obscured by notebooks, lies a cracked cellphone that feels familiar when David palms the device for a moment before putting it away. The third and deeper drawer is the only organized portion of the whole desk. Neat, systemized folders fill the back half of the drawer while more unopened packets populate the front half in stacks. This fits the same boring business as the first two but the perfect order of the files attracts David's attention.

All are alphabetized and in pristine condition. Some have people's names written on the tabs, the others bear the name of companies. Ian even has a file with his name and contains only a copy of his will which leaves everything to David should he survive his husband. There isn't a file with David's name. Sharing a last name means it should be right before Ian's but there is nothing to be found. Whose original last name is Flanigan? A quick perusal of what's written on the files turns up nothing that has David as a forename. The meager contents of all other files lose his attention when he discovers the thickness of a folder belonging to Jonathan E. D. Roman, Esquire.

. . .

The short hours between skimming the file until Ian comes home are spent in stilled silence. Not even his own shallow breathing dares to rise above a hushed whisper and break his concentration. His name being spoken out loud several times brings his attention to the other person in the room. Eyes lock and exchange similar expressions. Shock at being caught turns into embarrassment, which finally morphs into the resentment of betrayal. Neither dares to speak first. All David thinks to do is put the file back in its alphabetical place, close the drawer, get up and walk out of the room, right by Ian. Conviction dictates David not even wince or glance peripherally at the man he shrugs past and away from.

. . .

Night falls before David and Ian cross paths in the kitchen. Nibbling on leftovers, David can't answer Ian's question immediately. Ian is asked to repeat it once David swallows his food.

"Is there any of that left or is what you're eating the last of it?"

A rising upset is suppressed when Ian doesn't lead with a question or comment of concern about earlier. It stays dormant. A different approach: instead of getting incensed, David calmly asks the question to put the ball in volley so the game can begin.

"How long?" David's double worded question slips softly from between his lips but loud enough for Ian to hear with ease.

Ian hesitates for a moment, expecting an outburst of rage that never comes. "A while." His own double worded reply carries with it the same calm as the question it answers. There's no point in being provoked by an inescapable reality.

"Let's keep it vague," David insists, "but before my accident, right?"

"Yes."

"And are you still…"

"Yes."

David nods his acceptance. No new emotion comes, he already knows the truth. Paper trails replace his need to rely on the accuracy of words from Ian's mouth. Otherwise, David might easily be persuaded and tolerate more of Ian's self-serving candor. "Can I ask why?"

"He was there for me when you were in a coma. Nobody thought you'd make it, not even the doctors."

"But you were seeing him before that, though…"

"Yes."

"Were we getting a divorce before I had my concussion?"

"We were talking about it."

"Was he the reason I wanted to leave you?"

"No. He just became another reason."

"Did I know there was more than one?"

"I believe you did. I wasn't very good at hiding things back then."

"Just tell me whatever you want me to believe because I won't know any better. Rewrite the past to make the present and future however wonderful and edited you want."

"You were happy, weren't you?"

"I shouldn't have been."

"You deserved to be happy after what happened—"

"But it's a happiness you designed. Who even knows what I wanted. Certainly not this."

"I promise I thought it would be a good way to get us back

on track. Almost losing you made me realize how much I love you. And a second chance with the past out of the way was too good to be true."

"That usually means it is, Ian."

The question of why remains half-answered. Nothing more can be said. Too defeated before a real battle has a chance to begin, they both entered the conversation resigned to an obvious finale. Arguing won't solve problems or fix past failures. What's done has been done before David forgot his relationship was over.

Still, David wants to say more but stops. The reason he's here still hasn't revealed itself, at least not to him. A purpose exists beyond these four walls, David is sure. It'll be easier to figure out someplace where walls don't keep suffocating memories trapped while they fall in on themselves and their false sense of security.

"Did you take all my money?" David asks with trepidation, genuinely fearful of the answer.

"No. You still have most of it."

Stoicism suppresses a weary smile. "I'm going to sleep on the couch tonight," David states with sudden insistence.

Ian agrees with a little nod up and down before he retreats upstairs, so quiet for the night. The comfort of loneliness tastes bittersweet. Through an aggravating headache, David tries to focus on what to do the following day with so many available options to explore. One step at a time. Sleep first, dream later.

. . .

At least once a day, Ian wonders what was going through David's mind when the switch for all the power in his brain was turned off for the last time. Finding him dead on the couch with his eyes wide open suggests an opportunity to see death coming. The serene look haunts Ian and mocks him as a revenge against an unintended but calculated treachery. In the end, David found death a pleasant, viable option.

Ian and Jonathan deserve one another. When David was alive, weekly threats to expose Ian's infidelities kept alive what only one of them considered a relationship. Jonathan won and Ian lost. Any attacks on Jonathan's actions are met with a reminder of how Ian did essentially the same thing, just with a different approach. A marriage proposal including a prenuptial agreement always follows the lawyer's likely rebuttal. Jonathan mentions that he even expects Ian to cheat. He just hopes they will be together for life.

The nights when a proposal blesses the day bring David back to life in Ian's mind. More than any ordinary day among the scattered and scarce remnants of their previous relationship. The potentials of a living lover are overshadowed by what Ian believes with all his heart were David's aspirations before he died. As time went on, they included him less, Ian is certain. The prospect of David's life minus Ian was becoming obvious. The old David would've given up faith in any man, the dial of his resentment set permanently to high.

Sunlight shines on Ian's face in the mornings when the clouds allow. David loved it, so now Ian hates it. The symbolism means so little, lost on a man whose acquiescence to grief cripples his spirit. Anxiety, regret, remorse; so much joins forces to make him despondent. Echoes of past failures are evident all around him. And with the one person he thinks he still loves, he failed twice. Now to stumble through the rest of life unaware, unsure of its purpose or if one still exists. He thinks he understands the reason he was put on earth, but he knows better. He expects that he too will die like David, never realizing.

BOYS BEING BOYS

TAYLOR DAYNE understood and her timing was uncanny. She sang her shared hope for a lover over the low din of conversations between mostly coupled people. A delivery wasn't guaranteed for James but the song's message came as a sign. His friends predicted the rest of his life would be spent staring into the bottom of a glass. They had been right for the past two and a half years and each day made it easier for James to make it an eventual truth. He laughed at the thought as he tilted his head back to get the last drop of beer stubbornly tucked in the bottom crease. The thicker glass of the base glorified the colorful hues of the overhead lights. When the inside was completely dry, James closed his left eye, put the glass to the open right eye, and surveyed the room. Everybody looked still, except for their mouths that barely moved, humming like soft electricity. Then Eddie walked through the door.

Stumbled was more accurate. A slow shuffle moved him with caution to the closest empty seat at the bar, right next to James. An alarmed bartender stared at him suspiciously upon their simultaneous approaches to James's left. "Looks like you've had a few too many already. I'm going to call you a cab—"

"No, Terry. No need. He's with me," James said. "The Uber just dropped him off. Let us have at least one drink before we head out."

"Yeah, Terry. Let us have at least one drink before we head out," the stranger slurred.

"Okay, but he's your responsibility. If he gets out of hand at all, you're both out. I still don't think I should serve him."

The stranger leapt to his feet, startling everybody who cared to look. The perfect contender for a bootleg Marlon Brando: a tight, plain white t-shirt and well-worn denim jeans clung to his brutish, muscled body. Half of an angelic face snarled and hid behind a lush, dark mustache and beard. Curious brown eyes challenged anyone who stared long enough to extend any amount of sympathy. Reliance on those aspects alone was not enough to impress the onlookers A macho show of sobriety offered proof he could handle at least one more drink. Dropping to the floor, he began a series of one-armed pushups. With his free hand, he touched the tip of his nose then extended the arm and brought it back to again touch the tip of his nose. The rhythm matched the one-armed raising and lowering of his body, each action marked by a letter of the alphabet from Z backwards to A.

"So Terry," he said, once back in his seat, "gimme a shot of whisky and a glass of whisky. And my buddy here is gonna pay for it since I had to get the Uber."

An eager nod from James temporarily assuaged Terry's concerns.

"Thanks for that," the stranger said. "My name is Eddie. You should know that so our story comes off more convincingly."

"I'm James, and I should thank you," James said in reference to Eddie's demonstration. The compliment missed its mark. *Strike one,* James lamented. *And I only just learned his name.*

"Nah. Thank you for the whisky. I'll be out of your hair in a bit."

"Stay and talk as long as you like," James insisted and hoped it didn't come off too eager.

"Well, whisky ain't cheap in D.C., so sure. I owe you at least a few minutes of chit chat."

"More if you want. Don't worry about Terry kicking you out. Unless you got someone waiting for you someplace else."

Eddie exploded with laughter as Terry returned with the shot glass and the tumbler of whisky. "Nope. No place to go. Got kicked out tonight. I really think it's legit this time." The shot glass was expertly emptied down his throat and slammed back down on the bar as an exclamation point.

James saw it as a physical expression of Eddie's accepting defeat. "What are you going to do, then?" he inquired.

"Get a hotel, I guess."

"You don't have any friends? That'd be cheaper."

"Our friends were her friends, not mine. All my friends stopped talking to me after we started dating…"

James heard nothing but an insignificant string of words draped like an ugly necklace around *her* neck. His deepest desire at hearing about *her* was that Eddie would tighten the necklace around *her* neck like a garotte and squeeze until he choked all the breath from her lungs. Most of what Eddie said about his girlfriend and the possible demise of their relationship went unheard.

"You still with me?" Eddie asked, jerking James back into the conversation. "Never mind. It don't matter. I'll finish my whisky and get going."

With that, Eddie tilted head and hand backward and with a might two swallows, emptied the tumbler of whisky into his gut. Eddie offered a nod of thanks before he rose from the barstool to turn and walk back out into the night. He only made it five steps along the short path to the door when he stumbled and fell face first mere feet before the entrance.

James jumped to his feet. "I got him! Put it on my tab, Terry."

"Come back tomorrow and pay, James!" Terry demanded before the clamor from the curious onlookers rose to make any conversation inaudible.

Eddie's bulk was difficult for James's lanky frame to lift. The drunken dead weight became a terrifying burden to support. It would be best to try and revive him, but how would James wake Eddie? He was afraid to slap him, fearful of some half-expected violent retaliation. A glass of water poured from over James's shoulder and splashed in Eddie's face. Terry smiled with accepted guilt before walking back behind the bar. Eddie's eyes fluttered open but no other motion followed at first. After a moment of looking around to get his bearings, he picked himself off the floor in a flash of sobriety. Another moment was needed to acclimate and take in what he effectively could of his surroundings. Embarrassment kept him silent as he slowly walked the rest of the way to the door from where he had fallen.

"I got him!" James said pointlessly, since by then nobody cared about that situation anymore.

. . .

Ice clinking in an empty glass brought Eddie around. The noise pounded in his head and he winced at the light as it poured in through the cracks of his barely shut eyes. "Where the hell am I?" he wondered to himself but loud enough for James to hear. The voice asking thundered and dealt a cleaving blow to his brain. Thinking hurt. Opening his eyes only made the aching worse.

"Back with us?"

Eddie shut his eyes again, but kept his mouth open, hoping more oxygen held the power to heal. The loud reverberation of heavy glass colliding with heavier glass sounded in front of him. He opened his eyes to a glass of water, light with ice. "This ain't what I want," Eddie slurred.

"But it's what you're going to get," James returned.

Defeated by the authoritative tone of the response, Eddie guzzled the water, enjoying the refreshment in secret. "Now give me a real drink." Eddie asked more than demanded.

James took the empty glass away then returned with it again filled with water. "Two glasses of water per real drink. I don't want you choking on your own vomit once you pass out."

"But it's okay that I piss all over your couch?"

"Better than you dying on my couch."

The logic defeated Eddie's inebriated attempt at refusing the water so he once more gave in, thinking only of the drink that was sure to follow. To his delight, a whisky and soda, heavier on the whisky, came to him in a chilled tumbler. The first sips Eddie savored, but the rest he poured down his throat. After a minute the spirit possessed his limbs to make them numb and relaxed while his brain warmed and cooled at the same time. Condensation and clouds grayed his already overcast mind but it's what he preferred and wanted. Something terrible needed forgetting and he succeeded, feeling only the couch beneath him and the sleepiness that started its deliberate wash. Eddie soon would drown in something other than anger, regret, pain.

He welcomed its quick undertow and was swept away at last in slumber's drink.

James stared at Eddie with intent. The beautiful man lay sprawled across the entire length of the couch. James sat across from the sleeping beauty and pondered. First about how to make his guest comfortable as he eyed the blankets stacked behind the couch. Eddie's face appeared flushed and his brow damp. Blankets were out of the question. Then James thought to undress Eddie. Nerve-rattled limbs needed something soothing. James stood up, anxiously paced for a minute, and grabbed the tumbler from the table that once held Eddie's whisky soda.

The first shot of straight liquor went down rough, scorching a trail of repentance down the back of his throat and down into his stomach. The next shot was intended to calm his trembling extremities, but instead only encouraged another shot, along with a minor bump in ordinary courage. His head felt light so he sat for a moment, again across from Eddie. The rhythmic raising and lowering of the sleeping man's chest became the focus of James's own breathing. Their matched respiration lent James a deceptive sense of familiarity, of a closeness that never existed. *That can be changed,* James thought. He stood up and sat in the only accommodating space for himself on the couch near Eddie's hip. The closer proximity intoxicated an already fascinated imagination. The continued rising and falling of the drunk man's chest stretched the white cotton of his t-shirt. With their breaths again matching, James felt comfortable helping Eddie out of the confines of the restricting garment.

The shirt peeled off with ease. Drunken heaviness held no difficulty for fixated intention. With care, James placed his hand on Eddie's chest to feel his heartbeat. Slow and steady compared to his own which raced twice as fast. Heat transferred from skin to skin and James wanted to feel more mingling of that warmth. Removing his shirt, he nestled himself into the side of the sleeping body with its arms raised and inviting. Within seconds the warmth amplified and both bodies perspired into a collective dampness.

Standing up made James aware that his thighs also produced an uncomfortable sweat. He removed his pants quickly. The fictional conjoining of feeling convinced him that Eddie must also have the same dilemma. Sweaty palms pressed against either side of James' head to squeeze the tension of trepidation out. *He'll sleep better,* the drunken brain decided. With the same care and relative ease, the tight blue jeans came off the unconscious man. A satisfied sigh persuaded James that he did the right thing.

Another shot of alcohol later and James remembered why he went out to the bar in the first place. The objective was never to get drunk, but to bring home a guy. Too many months had passed since James had sex of any kind. Across from him, half-naked on his couch, rested the most beautiful man he'd seen in a while. Lean muscle gave shape to the arms, legs, chest and torso blanketed in a pelt of dark fur. Expertly cut hair faded into a well-kept beard and mustache. Eddie's white briefs bulged suggestively to match the mounds of muscled geography. But Eddie was straight. And recently out of a relationship. And completely passed out. And absolutely beautiful.

James hated that his mind went where it did, wondering how far either of them considered too far, drunk or otherwise. There existed between them no intimacy other than first names. More than enough for a gay man to have sex with another gay man. How much could James get away with under the justification of boys being boys? Did straight people subscribe to the casualness of sex with the same rampant, epidemic fervor? Throughout those and the many quandaries that followed, the concept of consent never entered the discussion. Certainly that notion wielded a heft that also carried potential legal retribution. In the end, Eddie became only a man to James, flesh and blood tenting both of their underwear. *What would Eddie do in a similar situation with an object of desire ready and easy to have, certain to remember nothing in the morning?* James couldn't help but wonder.

One final, tiny shot from the same glass that knocked Eddie out felt like a kiss from his lips. The liquid courage made James certain that one tiny brush against the real things with his own would be better than the sticky imprint on a glass. He sat close to Eddie's barely clad waist and gently leaned in for a brief kiss. For a straight man, Eddie had soft lips so another got stolen and locked away in a brain doomed never to properly remember.

Swooning, James braced himself with one arm against the back of the couch. His arm hovered over the sleeping body with the rising and falling of its labored life as proof of a desire for relief. James swore a heat could be felt charring the air and space between his limb and Eddie. He also swore to a sureness about much of the situation. Alcohol and desire made so much of the situation vague: flashes of black hair growing from pale skin on fire, the feel of flesh beneath fabric, the dark lettering of a common brand name printed around a waist band, more skin, more dark fur, and from what James determined, no opposition.

But something stopped James, the "what" less important than the "why." He knew the solution and the situation then would know only two ends: passed out somewhere or happy and face first in Eddie's lap. Drunk but amazed at how well the liquor held in his stomach, the drink kept him glistening in a truthful selfishness, one more tiny shot of whisky called the decision. Heat rose to his head and he barely made it into the chair before his legs gave out and buckled. The only way of conveyance between the small space separating him and his man for the night demanded it be traversed on all fours in both subjugation and genuflection. Preserving any concept of what happened afterwards was also made hopeless by a light head on fire.

...

James woke first and surveyed the room with eyes unusually adjusted for clear perception. The brain however stayed sluggish and processed little. What exactly happened? No messes needed tending to and nothing smelled out of sorts. More of the floor's hardness forced the parts of his body in contact with the timbers to match the supporting stiffness. Sitting up proved more difficult than necessary, standing upright nearly unmanageable. Blood and color drained from his head. James immediately returned to a seated position. He landed with little grace on a sliver of couch unoccupied by his still slumbering guest.

Little of the night before remained distinct. The single tumbler filled with a hardened puddle of whisky rested overturned on the table. With the sight of it came the smell, and with the smell came no recollection like James hoped. Looking over his right shoulder he had a close viewpoint of Eddie's hairy legs. Over his left laid a handsome face quite still in spite of the rise and fall of Eddie's powerful chest. Suddenly James remembered, the hypnotic motion of Eddie's breathing a trigger. No memories of actions sprang to mind, just leftover sensations of lust. A reticent smile barely had time to play on James's face before Eddie began to stir.

The proximity of a stranger so close to him startled Eddie. His head and body ached too much for a physical response, but the look on his face said enough. The man sitting next to his body stood up to give him more room to stretch and acclimate. Questions poured in to labor his head even more. What to ask first? Which was more important? Who or where? James's initiative to speak first pleased Eddie. Once the who and where became established, the why and what clamored to be understood next. A quick glimpse at his cell phone explained the why. *Now,* Eddie thought, *what the fuck happened? Why were we both in our underwear, hung over and so fucking close together when I woke up?* Volatile head and stomach aches warned that nothing would be learned without help from James.

The host presented the evening's events the best he could. Most of what James evoked from after the deluge of whisky received its information from impression alone, not actual memory. Before James spoke again, Eddie asked with sheepish insecurity: "Did you do anything gay to me while I was passed out?"

The manner of delivery contradicted the strength surely coiled in Eddie's burly, muscled body. The question knocked out any interest James had in him to tease or provoke the big half-naked straight boy on his couch. No proof manifested from a hasty examination of thoughts and any available physical evidence. Both woke up still in their underwear. Neither bore tell-tale stains or signs of distress. James could only speculate at the briny taste noticed in spurts whenever his tongue moved about the inside of his mouth.

"Absolutely not," James assured Eddie, who became instantly though only momentarily relieved.

Dressed and full-bellied, Eddie thought more about the future than whatever happened in the past while he talked over coffee with James.

"Where will you go?" James asked.

"I really don't know," Eddie admitted. "All my friends were her friends. Can't go to any of them and ask for a place to stay. So a motel, I guess."

"I mean…you could stay here…"

Eddie looked at James with a hint of mistrust. "I don't really know you, man."

"True. But I'm trustworthy. I brought you here and took care of you. I could've left you at the bar when Terry wanted to kick you out."

"True. But why? What did you get out of doing all that?"

"The chance to do a good deed. The chance to make a friend."

A letup in the back-and-forth prodded Eddie into reexamining his previous state of undress. After hesitation, he asked: "Did you take my clothes off last night? I'm asking because I usually don't sleep in my underwear. I sleep naked."

With no reluctance of his own, James confirmed he did. Eddie followed up with, "Why?"

"You were burning up and sweating through your shirt."

"But you knew I wasn't gay, right?"

"You made that very clear, yes."

"Okay. Good."

With a satisfied smile, James changed the subject back to temporary cohabitation, his tension unnoticed. "Besides, staying here for a week or so will help you save money. I won't charge you."

"What? No way! What do you get out of doing that, now?"

"The chance to do an even better deed. And the chance to become a better friend."

Eddie thought about the offer and weighed the options. A face that could become more familiar held greater appeal than the dismal solitude of a motel room. That threatened too much introspection and Eddie had no need for that then, at least not for a week or so. He agreed, pleased and swayed in the end with the money to be saved from seven plus days of free room and board.

"I don't have a lot of stuff," Eddie admitted, also mentioning all the furniture and appliances belonged to his ex, "just clothes, mostly. When can I bring them over?"

"Anytime. Do you have a car?"

"Yeah."

"Wanna do it now? Sooner is better than later."

"Yeah, sure."

"Okay. I have an extra parking pass. I can take you to your car if you want."

"Maybe not a good idea. It should be back at my ex's, if she didn't have it towed. I'll Uber."

They walked together to the front door of James's apartment. An awkward moment passed that ended in a failed hug and near fumbled handshake.

"Okay. See you soon," Eddie said.

"I'll be here."

Eddie started to pivot towards the door with his back fully turned to James for the first time in memory. He needed confirmation one last time. "You know I'm not gay and nothing gay is going to happen between us, right?"

James nodded in agreement and Eddie, placated at last, smiled and turned to leave. Before closing the door, he announced: "I'm going to get us a bottle of whisky to celebrate a new friendship."

James concealed the attitude that threatened to allow the reticence of his smile to fully form. "Get two," he insisted, "we killed my only bottle last night and I'm sure we'll need to replace it sooner or later."

TWO GOODBYES IN A DAY

He'd be lying through his crooked teeth if he tried convincing anybody that the fear of this day hadn't already made his eyes water, and more than once. Fresh donuts made to order waited more patiently for their fate than Jarman. Elián wasn't late, time just played its usual cruel joke. Of course it would, and why not? There were the memories with Elián to consider: hours of chatter, kisses and laughter became a common thread running through their encounters and binding them together. Jarman couldn't decide whether to ponder the past or fret about the uncertain future. Neither of the options were pleasant. In minutes Elián would arrive, ready for his donut After breakfast and conversation, kissing and groping over a TV show, they would make the inevitable trip upstairs to the bedroom.

The word celebration can't be used in reference to the sad occasion of saying goodbye. Surely Jarman, being a writer, knew a more sufficient word. Synonyms that morning held no importance. Sex always brought Jarman joy, a way to honor the desire felt between two wanting bodies. Impressions affected passion and misery suppressed libido. The desire would be there; a sturdy, young marine in his physical prime had such power over a man floating in his mid-forties. And the heat outside, when coupled with the promise of a southern summer, remained a principle of lust that inspired in him a unique sensuality. But would that be enough to provide Jarman with an erection? Sex might be difficult to make happen, and it might not have the same effect Elián hoped for. Then their last encounter would be marred and anticlimactic.

The unlocked door allowed Elián easy access to the house. Up the first flight of stairs, he saw Jarman's head turned in profile to greet him.

"Howdy handsome," Jarman welcomed.

"Hey!" Elián responded, a slight extension at the end of the word.

Jarman got up from the couch and crossed the living room to meet his friend. They embraced. For the first time that day, Jarman held on tight to him, hoping he could also hold on to time, or at least slow it down with his clinging weight. The return embrace suggested Elián's attempt at something similar. *He's not crazy like you,* Jarman reminded himself.

Next to each other on the couch, both wondered who would be the first to speak. Nerves kept both from saying anything sincerely on their minds, in spite of a yearlong familiarity. That intimacy made what the other was feeling easier to read. Indirect glances, fidgety gestures that served no purpose – these and other hilarious telltale signs made the contents of their heads outwardly clear. Indirect glances from each man served to capture the intimate details expressed on their faces, in the gray of Jarman's mustache and beard and the cursive script spelling Spanish words on Elián's muscled, furry arms. They amused each other with fidgety gestures that served no purpose. These and other telltale signs made the disjointed contents of their heads outwardly clear. A hand placed with care on Elián's leg announced Jarman's intention to speak first. It made sense with him being more impulsive and impetuous. But he spoke only a choked hello. This made Elián smile. Finally staring into each other's eyes for more than a second, they kissed. Passion and an impending departure insisted it last longer than a usual welcoming kiss.

Trepidation stained the hours leading up to the possibility of them having sex. Stress, work, the state of the world, depression, all conspired to blemish what Jarman and Elián anticipated as an obvious part of their farewell. This was a concern Jarman expressed when plans were made over texts. A formidable melancholy grew into the worst threat. One full year until Elián returned from being stationed in the middle east.

Elián's mouth on his mouth charged an internal voltage that demanded all of Jarman's straying attention, shocking it back to the moment. Burning veins melted inside equally heated flesh. Within minutes of kissing, Jarman peeled off his shirt before helping Elián out of his. A sincere look distributed between them and in that split second, they understood their parallels, recognized as shared and accepted. At the forefront was longing. The rest would be dealt with later. When their lips and tongues met again, Jarman opened his eyes into thin slits with the belief it afforded him extra snapshots of Elián's youthful face.

It wasn't long until they were spent, lying naked, wrapped in warm legs and arms. The practice of holding on to each other for dear life continued. Jarman loved the confirmation of Elián's extended effort. The ambition to drag time down became his solitary concern. No effort of concentration kept neglected worries from knocking on windows, breaking them all open and screaming further demands, a tantrum at its excessive and petulant finest. How full the moments seemed before the brittle shell that protected the embryonic center cracked open. This added to the list of past presents that were opened, acknowledged, and discarded.

Cleaned and clothed, they continued to hold each other over the course of the dialogue that followed, idle and casual talk, like the way they lounged together on the couch. Fake but harmless fronts protected raw feelings from being exposed. Each knew what the other hid, a mirror image of reciprocal stares. Elián wanted to ask why Jarman's usual playful teasing lacked bite, the quick wit dulled to a blade hardly able to cut warm butter. The same question could be asked of Elián in return but no need. There was already so much cause for heartbreak.

Elián's disarming smile made Jarman forget the future, so underscored with ambiguity. The past would be better recalled some other time. Conversation continued its prior posturing: this was a day just like any other. But so much was already altered. Jarman loved Elián more under the threat of absence. Not in love, but the affection and consideration that came from an accumulation of several years of friendship. Yet they barely knew each other a full year. They applauded themselves as validation that the journey shared the same importance as the end.

Their planned hours advanced. The inexorable subject of Elián's deployment crept into the conversation. He had already been told but Jarman needed reminding. The recap was brief. Going to Bahrain in two weeks, on July fourteenth, for a whole year. Hearing the words in person made the imminent departure definite. Jarman swore at that moment he felt a rip in the narrow space separating his body from Elián's warmth. Any attempt to fuse the parts of themselves together offered a temporary fix, at best. There was sad music to face. The curtain remained down to obscure the backstage action behind

Jarman's brave show of emotions, a triumph. He kept his eyes closed just in case.

The minutes that remained were too few and impossible to keep trapped inside a tight fist. More people waited for their turn to try and hold onto Elián in desperation, until they also needed to let him go. The two men couldn't bring themselves to say any of the prepared words. If cliché phrases got thrown around then the sorrow of the situation would declare victory and win, satisfied with any scarring left in its wake. The varnish of stoicism needed to be intact for a memorial service being held in a couple hours. Elián too had more people to see. Possibly, he would never cross paths with them again either. Its own kind of memorial service

Outside, the sun shone down on the two men with growing ferocity. The all-seeing eye watchful while punishing.

Jarman joked about legitimate concerns, hoping to lessen their impact.

"Glad I wasn't too depressed to do everything we wanted to do," Jarman confessed.

"Even if we didn't," Elián started in earnest, "I wouldn't have cared. I just wanted to see you. Mission accomplished. And no matter what we did or didn't do all the times we hung out before, I have never been disappointed hanging out with you." Jarman concurred openly with a kiss. Arms firm around each other lacked the earlier urgency of past embraces. No more pretending time was something tangible and malleable. A middle-aged man like Jarman knew better. So did a slightly seasoned marine of twenty-five.

Another day and soon, another state, and then another country, and finally, another time. With a kiss and hug that both wished were never ending, the fearful word at last fell from their mouths, simultaneously so nobody had to carry the burden of being the first, or of appearing eager to see the other off.

"I know we'll see each other again," Jarman said with shaky and mustered bravura.

"We will," Elián confirmed.

The facile and infectious optimism reassured Jarman. "Exactly," he said to seal the deal. "Besides, this is just the end of a chapter, not the book." The writer in him never could keep craft references out of conversations.

Elián laughed. "Exactly. Which is why we don't need to draw this out any longer. We both have other places to be."

Jarman agreed with a sharp swat to Elián's ass.

"I can't wait to get to the part in the book where we see each other again," Elián stated.

"Me either. You be safe, sergeant."

"I will if you will."

"I'm staying put. Nothing's gonna happen to me."

How presumptuous, Jarman thought as the words escaped his mouth.

A final kiss to last the rest of the year and well into the next had to be significant, damn near earth-shattering. Neighbors outside were unlucky enough to see homosexual men kissing while affection, infatuation and tongues fueled the action. In broad daylight. Just past noon, a few staid onlookers pretended not to notice, even when loud proclamations of love were exchanged.

"I love you, Elián"

"I love you, Jarman."

"I'll see you next year in New York when you come home."

"That's a promise."

"It sure is. One more quick kiss…you know I like to piss off the neighbors."

Afterwards, Elián got into his car, started the ignition, and began to back out. Each waved and finally looked away, towards the rest of the day ahead. Jarman surprised himself by not crying before either had the chance to look away from one another.

There was an initial difficulty switching gears. Jarman felt a hot shower might help rinse lingering emotional residue from the first half of his day. Symbolism meant a lot and an act of ablution needed to involve water of some kind. The second half of the day presented its own challenges. Fatigue was already a threat and the dangerous heat outside guaranteed to make Jarman more sluggish.

There were scattered thoughts to collect and organize into a cohesive tribute to a woman Jarman met in person only twice. He had a couple days to prepare some semblance of a speech. Eric, son of the deceased, didn't want anybody religious so his good friend, the writer, was the next best thing. *A better thing,* Jarman offered in response. A solemn eloquence coursed through his usual work and lent itself well to a brief sermon about the value of life being measured in memories. Nothing else mattered or was left at the end. These and other possible random, haphazard thoughts were put together into a formal, linear stream of consciousness and finalized during the half hour car ride to Eric's house.

The marked difference of emotions and deliberations allowed to run free startled Jarman until he wrangled them into a presentable eulogy. Understandably, feelings about Elián surfaced, some of which were comparable, almost interchangeable with certain meditations about the other departure of a human being. Whether a person passed through someone's life or passed from that life, the finality became the end of a chapter. The past forty-eight hours saw the transference of sentiments between the two episodes. Remorse, regret… unhappiness wove a tapestry that blanketed Jarman, suffocating yet insulating.

The writing seemed too hasty in its construction; the intent came across as dubious. Short notice held little blame as Jarman thought back on when he produced twenty times as much in a shorter span of time. His opinions were genuine, it was an eventuality that he would cry. Concern centered on whether what was written supported attitudes intended for Eric's mother. A second read through made the words come off like regurgitated sentimentalities since Jarman hardly knew the deceased. Everyone else certainly had mountains of memories to bury Jarman's diminutive contribution in a breathtaking avalanche of tributes. Should he open with famous Prince lyrics? Would it be inappropriate to mention she thought Jarman had great abs?

He arrived late to the house greeted by several faces he didn't know. Understandable when Jarman again considered he barely knew the deceased, her husband, or even her other son, Eric's brother. People kept filing in to provide a larger turnout than Jarman expected. The handful he thought would attend tripled, with the larger contingent lingering inside, free from the overbearing sun. Within a minute of arrival, he saw Gwen, Eric's wife, who whisked him away to her bedroom.

"Close the door," she instructed. Once she heard the door shut, she opened the drawer of a bedside nightstand that held her gaze since the moment she sat on her bed. A joint was lit. Gwen took the inaugural puffs, then offered it to Jarman. "Thank you for doing this for us. And on such short notice."

Jarman remained standing and spoke after he exhaled. "My pleasure, though that response doesn't seem appropriate right now. But you know what I mean."

"I do and I thank you. It means a lot to us, Eric especially."

"You all mean a lot to me. Y'all know I'd do damn near anything for you guys."

For a minute, the joint was smoked and passed in painful silence. Heavy hearts full of too much desolation inside them both.

"How was your morning?" Gwen inquired.

"Pretty uneventful," Jarman lied. He saw no need to add to the grief already in the air. Both wanted the smoke filling the room to banish any negativity not subdued by shifting focus elsewhere. Another joint appeared right as Jarman smashed the butt of the first in a half-filled ashtray. He thought of his impending, unsure soliloquy, about the heat that threatened him with both burns and exhaustion, and in the end, of how tired he already was. Distress menaced a mind already unstable and fogged by further smoking. Jarman remembered he was a professional. There were innumerable engagements when he had to speak longer and under worse conditions.

Less small talk made over the second joint meant it finished quicker. And just in time. Another guest opened the door to announce that the service was ready to begin. Most people were already outside when Gwen and Jarman made their way through the house.

Eric stood up front and started an informal opening when

he saw his wife and friend emerge from the backdoor onto the patio. Any remaining stragglers spilled out behind them. "Thank you everybody for coming, really. It means a lot to me, and my family and it would mean a lot to my mom if she knew all of you were here in her honor."

Eric continued, briefly outlining the loose structure of the service. Jarman guzzled an entire bottle of water between stepping outside and being called up to speak. The heat initiated its visible punishment on the crowd.

Don't mess this up. The mantra spoken, Jarman was free to begin and as usual, heeded his own warning. A clear intonation presented to everyone how deeply felt his vocabulary was and what an honor it had been to meet her those couple of times. Ruminations on people's importance to an individual's life culminated with a plea to not focus on past incongruities, but to better focus on why people are worthy of remembrance and tribute. Again, since memories are what people become after they're gone, departing as the best memory possible should be a venerated endeavor. Jarman's cognizance of these poetries made him choke back tears. A proper send-off was what his prepared speech gave. Combined with the other off-the-cuff tributes to a life that meant so many different things to myriad people, the deceased received exactly what she deserved. The effect enlivened the group, despite being drained by the sun and the heat.

"I feel bad seeing a lot of you noticeably melting right now. Please continue to share your stories with anybody and everybody, but let's officially end the speaking outside and get some cold beers."

Jarman joined the migration indoors for another cold

bottle of water and the relieving shade of four walls and a roof. Gwen again found Jarman.

"Come with me," she called when she walked past, and once back inside her room, she continued: "Thank you again, Jarman. What you said was beautiful. And not religious, so thank you for that also."

Jarman thought back on what he said only a half hour ago. The slight jangle of nerves, the overbearing heat and the two joints they smoked made him slip into autopilot. He apologized for not making it more personal but reiterated he and Eric's mother only ever met twice in person.

"Don't worry about it, what you said and how you said it were perfect. And she thought a lot of you so the fact that you said anything at all would've thrilled her to death...you know what I mean."

Jarman nodded.

"And she'd be happy that everyone here is having a good time, smoking and drinking. Exactly how she would've wanted her life to be celebrated."

Immediately Jarman's mind snapped from processing Gwen's acclaim back to an earlier thought from the first part of his day. In particular, the one about goodbyes being celebrations. Boisterous laughter and hints of stories about Eric's mom sounded through the walls and closed door of the bedroom. He stood corrected.

Forty-three trips around the sun taught him much about loss, its various guises and consequences. Not every instance became a forlorn occasion, or even had to be. But Jarman practiced the childish habit of wanting everyone and everything deemed important to be a part of him forever and to never

ever change. He knew better, but it was a challenge to let go. Or to accept certain changes, at the very least. Sad goodbyes could also be festive. For this memorial service, an inebriated revelry sent Eric's mother off into an unknown after life. For Elián, an orgasm replaced the adieu and came with the promise of another one to be shared in another year.

Jarman began to accept happier farewells. Small talk with the flow of people in and out of the bedroom to smoke kept his mind from regressing. Instead, he listened and only spoke when spoken to. An ecstatic wave of humility washed over him. Everybody's lifted spirits made time pass faster than it should have. As the swells began to lessen with the light of the day, the reserves of Jarman's energies ebbed in response.

The full extent of Jarman's sapped batteries didn't reveal itself until he got home and sank into his couch. The scent of Elián's cologne still floated light in the air. The odor of too many joints clung stubbornly to his clothes. Already a day measured in memories, immaculate in spite of deep roots in the muddy quagmire of the events.

An ephemeral stream of tears came, slow and few, down his face and into his graying mustache. Relief from two successful performances swelled his chest and left him as a mighty exhale of gratitude. For the opportunity of having a friend and lover in Elián, temporarily gone but not forgotten, he offered praise to whoever dared accept it. And whoever still listened heard Jarman thank Eric's mother for giving life to an amazing friend. She too was gone, but certainly not to be forgotten anytime soon. Her son and Jarman shared more chances for memories to quantify how well they lived. In the same way that Jarman and Elián had finite but unexpired opportunities for their own memories.

Another shower before bed washed away the grime and sweat from outside. Slumber would come fast then stay through the night. Reading helped him fall asleep but was unnecessary that night. The rejected bedtime ritual made him think of books. Then, the analogy he made earlier to Elián, who most of the day occupied the bulk of his gray cells. The end of the book remained in the future. Tomorrow another page would be turned. A new chapter waited. Two supporting characters left but new people promised to find their way into the story, providing tension or relief, sorrow or joy. The privilege of having the book excited Jarman, especially with so many words left to read and experience.

TAKUSHĪ NO GŌSUTO

SIGNS OF transition were everywhere. Cranes moved with precision as they lifted, swiveled, stacked, turned, and repeated in day-long loops. "This place will never be back to the way it was, not in my lifetime." Oji-san liked to say this with more repetition than the machines tasked to rebuild. If he continued, it meant that the day was busy, and he was going to be in one of his moods. "And in your lifetime, the next one will come along to take this city right back to where it started, or gods forbid, much worse." Oji-san had always been cantankerous, but for the past four years it'd gotten more severe.

And if he continued with that angry mood, I'd try to stay out and take all the passengers I could fit in a day. That was less that I had to hear about how dissatisfied he is with everything, not to mention the disappointment he shares with my parents. I dropped out of school. I don't have the brains for what my parents want me to do, and they know it. To make them happy, I came here to Ishinomaki because Oji-san needed help. He lost everything in 2011: his beloved wife, and most of his friends. But his taxi business survived in a building reconstructed where the old structure stood. Having a relative around gave him some consolation and an extra body to burden. If I wasn't going into the business of my father, my punishment was a job in another family business.

"Naoki, you're like your father," Oji-san would say whenever I did anything wrong. His demeanor could give way to one even more critical, almost like he was finally able to boss around his imperious older brother, albeit a younger copy. All the more reason to stay out and drive the cab.

The air from the sea cleared my head when I needed to think, which I could do with all the hours driving, carrying passengers to and from wherever. Most trips were short so the need for any conversation beyond topical small talk didn't exist. Besides, most people found their own quiet time in my cab was a rare opportunity to let down their guard quietly, for their own private moment of silent respite. I was grateful because before long I'd get lost in my thoughts, wondering about what to do with my life. Being still new to town meant I still had much on my mind. But that day I tried my best to keep an empty head; no thoughts meant no worries and a day like that was needed once in a while.

Just past noon found me close to where the ocean meets the Kyukitakami River. Two tourists wanted to be taken from the Ishinomori Manga Museum to Hiyoriyama Park. Another short jaunt, thankfully. I decided that afterwards I would park and eat lunch in my cab. I wasn't too hungry, but I thought it better to get it out of the way, to free up more time for work. Oji-san was in a good mood, so I didn't have those reasons to stay out and drive. I just wanted to keep my head clear, my focus on however much nothingness I could grasp. The gracious passengers tipped well, the sign of tourists. What they lacked in wordiness they made up for with exuberant gratitude. Waving as I backed up, a flash of another person too close to the car caught my eye. I panicked and slammed on the breaks. I was only at 8 kilometers per hour, but the tires screeched as I halted. On the pavement, my startled former passengers flinched then demanded to know if I was okay. They clearly didn't see my next customer in their fluster of alarm. Neither did I until it was almost too late. They walked off when they realized nothing terrible happened. The next commuter slid into the car and silently closed the door.

A whiff of damp clothing hit my nose as I caught his reflection in the windshield mirror. The young man in the backseat nodded his acceptance of my smile. "Where to?" I asked, starting the meter. The answer came after an uneasy silence. Melancholy rode on the air of his fragrance. Humidity caused a light fog on the window next to him. His destination was Kamaya, a nearby town. I knew the town, and it could be reached in just over a half hour, roughly twenty-two kilometers away. My lunch could wait, I decided. I still wasn't very hungry.

The heaviness of unhappiness hung in the air and rode with us as I drove. Every time I looked at the young man in the backseat in the windshield mirror, I felt the urge to look again, then again, until I watched him more than the road. Confusing me further was a desire to speak with the silent passenger, whose gaze remained fixed in the direction of his feet.

"Kage," he said, as if he heard me wondering out loud to know more about him.

"I'm Naoki." I took his lead and offered only my first name. "Pleased to meet you."

He returned formalities then resigned himself inward to his previous calm. I still had questions even if I didn't know why or even where they came from.

"Do you live in Kamaya?"

"No." Kage's response started slow. "My friend works there."

"Ah, okay. You're going to visit a friend. Not the best day for it but at least it stopped raining. But there's not really much else to do. Thank the gods it stopped raining. It's still too cold, though."

I surprised myself by how chatty I became. Did I think the longer trip made me want to talk more? Maybe. But it didn't give me permission. However, something about Kage's hushed attendance that I couldn't quite figure out became the main reason. Kage gave me a polite smile in exchange for my bout of small talk. A terrible shyness choked back any return he could offer. After thinking about a better approach for ten minutes, I decided to reel it in if I expected him to open up and be more interactive. At that moment my stomach growled and gave me my next topic for conversation.

"Meeting your friend for lunch?" I asked.

The hesitancy remained as Kage began his response. "Yes," he started, "well, he was supposed to meet me at the park, but he didn't show up." Another intermission before he continued, this time more fevered. Apprehension tinged Kage's progress. "I called his cell phone, but it always goes right to voicemail. And I called his job but there's never an answer. It just rings and rings."

The longer he talked, my awareness of a wet, earthy smell increased. By that point in our trip, we were fresh upon the road leading directly to Kamaya. With the Oppa River to our right and the much larger Kitakami River on our left, the smell made sense. And considering Kage's clothes must've still been soggy from the rain earlier, any reason to explain became unnecessary. This understanding didn't make it any less unpleasant.

Kage's anxiety became even more apparent by the time he finished.

"I'm sure there's a good reason. You'll see."

"He was supposed to meet me at the park. I'm always the one who's late, not him."

"What's his name, if I may ask?"

"Taiyō."

The curious practice of not giving family names was not unusual to me. I respected Kage's desire for anonymity.

"You two must be good friends. Almost like it's you were destined to be."

Kage immediately withdrew inward again. I had to do my best to keep him in the conversation so I could know more. My puzzling curiosity demanded it.

"I only meant because of your names. Without the sun we don't have shadows. Can't have one without the other."

"But the sun doesn't need the shadow in order to exist," Kage solemnly returned. His retreat was almost complete. I had to change the subject but stay on course.

"What does Taiyō-san do?"

"He's a teacher. At an elementary school."

"That's great," I said with earnest sincerity.

Kage responded with what had become his usual slight nod and smile.

"I bet he loves it. I was going to school, but dropped out. I didn't like it much. Taiyō-san was on the other side of the room but honestly, I'm sure I wouldn't like that part of school either. Teaching, I mean…"

Finally, a wider smile forced to bloom by emotion broke open his mouth.

"He loves it."

Thankful for the advance, I struggled with what to say next, desperate for Kage to continue. It turned out he didn't need further nudging.

"Those kids are his life," Kage continued. "They've kept him at school late a few times before, more than I'd like, but I love how devoted he is to them all."

I noticed a spark in Kage's eyes and a swelling of pride in each word used to describe his friend. An inquisitive glare streaked across my face; had either of us blinked, neither of us would've seen it in the windshield mirror. But both of us saw my face and it had the opposite effect from what it intended. A shameful sorrow muted what delight had colored. Anger from something secret erupted from Kage, not as violence but as an absolute dimming of the light and briefly improved atmosphere. My profuse apologies did little to bring Kage back closer to his previous temperament. Whatever it was that upset him made the rest of the ride morose.

It became unclear which of us was more upset at first, until tears started to stream down Kage's face. "I need to see Taiyō!" he nearly screamed. His urgency alarmed me. We had reached Kamaya by then, so I asked him where to go next. This made his tears worse to the point where I thought his clothes were in danger of getting drenched again. "I don't recognize anything anymore." His confession barely made it through the sobs.

Though confused by his revelation, I didn't stop the car. Kage's unsure instructions prevented me from speaking until we turned onto a narrow, half-paved path that must have been a road at one time. At the end grew the ruins of an enormous building. As we approached, only the skeleton stood and like other things associated with the earthly remains of something tragically ended, sadness stared back and gave me reason to pause. I stopped the car, but Kage didn't seem to notice. He had closed his eyes and lowered his head.

"This can't be it," I whispered.

"It is!" Kage said, a dash of excitement back in his voice.

This only added to my confusion. I wanted to ask what he saw and what he heard, because I heard only the wind blowing through the bare bones of an empty building. Kage smiled and looked around as if the air was filled with the echoing laughter of children. I saw cold, gray concrete that by some miracle survived the worst tsunami this area had ever witnessed. Despite the day being overcast, light glinted in his eyes. Who or what was he seeing?

"Drive closer!" he demanded with excitement.

I followed his instructions and when I got too close for my own comfort to the shell of the building, I stopped again. No sooner had I done so, Kage threw open the door and jumped out, ran a few feet toward the building then froze. He gawked, his mouth hanging open, like the destruction happened in the blink of an eye.

"What is this?" Kage asked with slow deliberation of the words, as if what he was saying also couldn't be believed.

I got out of the car and stood next to him, my eyes darting between his face and the imposing, gutted structure. Words flooded my head, but they refused to be wrangled into anything intelligible. All I could do was watch as Kage's disorientation brought about more tears. For the first time since picking him up I could see him clearly, from head to toe. Much of his appearance was nondescript for someone his age and his clothes were either black or dark gray. Not only did his shadowy garments harmonize with his forename but his prevailing somber demeanor reinforced its suitability. Finally, his gloom became contagious and invaded me with a sense of grief.

"Nobody's here," Kage stated. Then, before I could say anything, "Taiyō's not here…"

Anything I said wouldn't have been consoling, even if it was comprehensible. One thing started to become clear but the more I thought about it the less it made sense.

The melancholy young man continued to stare at the vacant ruin.

"Kage-san, may I ask you a question?" My sudden ability to focus astonished me.

Kage didn't answer, he only looked away from the destroyed school towards me with tears pooled in his eyes.

I didn't wait for permission to continue. "What year is it?" My question made little sense to either of us.

Kage shook his head left to right.

"Kage, I think you're—" I started, afraid to tell him the truth, but he didn't want to hear out loud what he himself just started to realize.

Instead, he began to repeat: "I need to see Taiyō! I need Taiyō!" The volume of these two sentences grew louder until he was shouting, and they became a deafening roar. As abruptly as he had begun, a sudden quiet conquered everything. Even the wind knew not to blow anymore. Then, barely above a whisper, Kage said, "I love you, Taiyō."

Confessions lighten the burden of secrets and an admission in public lessens any shame attached to the hidden truth. The clouds allowed the sun to peak at the shadow boy and dry his tears. Bathed in those rays, the dark, faded colors of his clothes took on a brighter appearance. Then, perhaps even more brilliantly than the sun, the light in his eyes ignited. It became obvious to me in an instant: He finally saw his own sun, this Taiyō. All I could see was Kage. The smile on his face beamed as he faded away like that brief recess from the overcast day. Unsure of what to do next, I stood still and waited for the damp, clammy scent of my former passenger to disappear just as he had, completely and without a trace of even being there in the first place.

The drive back to the dispatch station took just over thirty minutes. Of all the things to ponder, what occupied my mind the most should've been the least important. What about the cab fare? Who was going to pay? Before we start a trip, it's logged in at the dispatch station once the meter is started. Whoever worked the computer knew that I had a trip from Ishinomaki to Kamaya. This trip was the furthest I'd gone all day with at least half of the shift still left. In addition, the amount of money handed over needed to match the trips a driver made that day. Oji-san became angriest over matters of money, stingy to the point of miserliness. The more I thought about a solution, the more confused I became. There could be no way to convince Oji-san that I gave a ride to a ghost.

The occasional trace of Kage's damp presence did little to alter my thoughts on the missed fare. The windows were rolled up so the closeness of the two rivers couldn't take the blame. For a second, I began to think it might be him trying to return, but then I asked myself why. He found his friend, his sun, his Taiyō. Since he couldn't find him on earth, no reason to return existed, even if Taiyō came along. They were together at long last. And I helped. The exhilaration that filled my soul was shocking. But a calm overtook me when I thought their contentment. Immediately, I decided I would pay the fare. This could be a way to finalize the act of kindness, to close the circle of accomplishment.

The closer I got to the dispatch station, the decision of whether to tell Oji-san what happened or not became less important. The experience was mine. Should I ever tell anyone? I'd be called crazy or a liar, so I resorted to keeping it a secret. I'm still new to town and don't need a reputation. People already knew me as Oji-san's nephew, that was sometimes hard enough to contend with.

Oji-san met my request to take the rest of the day off with a scowl. He never asked why, only for the money. Almost forgetting to include Kage's fare, Oji-san had another reason to interrogate, but he resisted. The look of disbelief he threw my way needed no interpretation. He knew my forgetfulness had nothing to do with the dishonesty of theft, but he detected something odd about the circumstances and my nervous behavior.

"Naoki, are you feeling okay?"

This unexpected sincerity startled me.

"Of course, Oji-san. Why do you ask?"

Oji-san stared at me as it to warn me against trying to lie to him.

"Can we go somewhere private to talk?" I asked.

He led me to his tiny office in the very back of the station. He sat at his desk and motioned me towards the chair across from him. I kept quiet for the first minute, unsure how to say what I knew I wanted to tell. Finally, it all came spewing out, but I was careful to include details about Kage's physical appearance, my emotions, our dialogue and his disappearance.

After I regurgitated the entire contents of the encounter, I looked at Oji-san directly, expecting backlash for wasting his time with a ghost story. And one that wasn't even scary. Instead of a string of insults, the left corner of his mouth raised a little and he nodded.

"You've been here four weeks now, right? I honestly expected something like this to happen to you sooner."

"I don't understand."

"Yes, you do. It's just like you said. You gave a ride to a ghost."

That realization I arrived at a while ago, and I told him so.

"We've all given rides to ghosts."

At this revelation, all I could do was sit and stare. How could it be easier for me to believe I saw a ghost but not believe someone else did, too?

"That's right. You're not special," Oji-san said. His trademark bite returned but this time it lacked the usual venom. "But what you did was respectable. Thank you for that."

Before I could make a joke and tell him he's welcome that I made sure he didn't lose any money, he continued.

"My gratitude has nothing to do with the money."

Did he read my mind?

"What you did was honorable and a beautiful service to the memory of those dear boys. I have no doubts that they found on the other side a separate peace they needed in order to love since it wasn't easy for them here on earth."

A tear streamed down Oji-san's cheek. He failed to wipe it away before I saw it. His bottom lip trembled as he spoke.

"I hope the same for me and your Oba-san because here on earth, I have nothing to live for," Oji-san said, at last admitting his defeat. His belief in the verity of that statement troubled me. "Strong bonds are no match for the gods. What she and I wanted, they didn't."

A determined spirit pervaded most of the city as it promised to rebuild and rise up stronger than before. There were many broken links, many people and buildings gone without time or chance to say goodbye. The chain was in pieces but never lost its purpose. Besides, it could always be reconnected with new bonds further strengthened by an indomitable spirit, not to mention their shared experiences and memories.

"Oji-san," I started, not really sure what to say next.

"Yes?" he replied without looking up at me, his head still low.

"Thank you." A deep bow accompanied my unprepared expression.

I ridiculed myself for what sounded like a desire to say something profound or comforting but which fell short at the last second. There was a slice of legitimacy in my scorn which made me wish I had something better to say. Oji-san had been described as stubborn, grumpy, abrasive, mean…the list never ended. That day was the first day I saw him cry. And somehow my expression of appreciation, no matter how flimsy I perceived it, moved Oji-san to shed fresh tears.

"Thank you," he said, bowing in return. "It's nice to have family around again."

What a perfect moment for a quick break in the clouds for a bit of heavenly and divine validation of the moment, but nothing. The need had been unwarranted once another miracle took place. Oji-san smiled as he stood up, walked around the desk and over to me. He rested his hand gently upon my shoulder.

"Have you eaten lunch yet?" he wished to know.

"Not yet."

"Good. Let's have lunch together."

A nod and a smile of my own meant yes. "My treat," I insisted, bending forward at the waist.

Oji-san bowed.

SHITFACED

FUCK…FUCK…Fuck! My head hurts…I want to get up and turn off the lights and go back to sleep but there's no switch for the sun. My brain is an anvil and something keeps hammering away inside. The pain and noise are maddening. Adjustment to the waking world comes slow to my bloodshot eyes. Yet more pain shoots through their sockets as sunlight brightens the agony alive in my skull. My other senses are also shot to hell. What did I drink last night? I've been drunk many times, in various degrees, and I can tell this isn't the hangover from too much alcohol. Unless I drank every bottle in the bar. So, shitfaced and maybe I smoked a bunch more weed on top of whatever I had to drink. Maybe it'll come to me.

I hear the presence before I feel it. A naked arm connected to a naked man – a quick grope informs me through my still closed eyes. A snore becomes a little laugh and that precedes his voice.

He declares: "I'm ticklish," then continues, "besides I hoped you'd wake me up like *this*…"

His hand grips mine at the wrist and guides it between his legs. Heat from his erection surges up my arm but stops at my heart before it gets the chance to go any further. That old thing saves the day again, intercepting before anything scores. My current frame of mind repulses me. The last thing I need right now is sex. My brain can't make any decisions if my heart's not in it.

I feel the shifting of his position on the bed as he turns

THURSDAY, MARCH 27
6:00-
9:00

STALKING HORSE PRESS AUTHORS & FRIENDS

AN AWP OFF-SITE EVENT WITH READINGS FROM

Jordan A. Rothacker
Jennifer Maritza McCauley
Jarrod Campbell
Genevieve Betts
Karen Gaul Schulman
Austin Eichelberger
Scott Daughtridge Demer

Creature Comforts Brewing
1124 San Julian St.

over. "Good morning handsome," he coos, continuing his sluggish seduction.

I respond by fluttering my eyes open. The light is excruciating and completes the job of splitting my head in two. Blindness gives way to a hazy view of who's lying next to me. My eyes slow down their blinking before settling into a deep squint before they close. When my sight returns, the furious blinking begins again. The shape of his head, blurred before, reveals a face only a mother could love. Immediately I think about my own mom, and how she still loved my brother, despite his being ugly inside and out. The boy beside me is just not attractive at all. His long face gives room for a large, stretched nose that owns most of the space. It flattens as he smiles. Asymmetrical eyebrows form crooked arches over a stare meant to be a part of his attempt to entice. I close my eyes again to shut out his face and its illumination by the awful yellow sunlight. There are now two things I'm not ready to see this morning.

I swear what feels like at least a half hour passes before I roll over and slowly open one eye first, just to peek, then the other, to make sure I can deal with either the face or the winter morning sun. His face is closer than before, but the same inviting smile remains smeared across it. Cute haircut, though. Laying on top of the covers, the full expanse of his body displays the reason I must've overlooked such an unpleasant face. The possibility that he drugged me remains. But his body, stretched out with one arm cocked and that hand supporting his head as he looks at me with a goofy expression…it's extraordinary. With him elongated, I'm given the most spectacular presentation of his taut musculature. How his form must have looked stretched and bent during sex. I now want to fuck, with all my heart. His eyes dart to the general location where my hand lands as it slips under the sheets. A tell-tale motion from my now obscured arm brings him satisfaction, too. When I pull back the sheets to show him my own excitement growing between my legs, that fulfillment matches my dick's progress. The invitation he is waiting for.

Hairy calves squeeze against my hips once he's straddling me. He seems surprised and I'm not sure why. I can't see what my face looks like. Hell, I'm barely aware of anything besides the boy grinding on my lap and the still unsurmountable pain pounding away in my head and keeping time with our fucking. I imagine his startled look is a reaction to one of my own. I'm astonished that my head is making sex even possible. The impulse clearly said, "fuck it" to visiting my big head and went right to the little one to straighten the situation out and have its way. And it lasts just as long as we both want and expect. Smiles all around, even if doing so almost kills my shivering brain.

Coffee with Irish cream helps my headache immensely. Reintroductions are necessary, so is a reminder of what part of town I'm in at present. There were a couple bars my friends and I had on the list last night, so I wonder out loud which one claims the honor of being where we met. The sentiment pleases him, which I find funny considering it houses no real excitement. Great care is taken to not show off my own complete lack of authenticity. Turns out he likes it. Our backstory gets recounted in suspicious detail. He remembers so much because he can hold his liquor better, he tells me. Even what comes off to me as a future challenge can't make the thought of spending another night out drinking appealing. With anyone, not just him. During a lull in our conversation, I offer to take him out for a late breakfast.

Christ, Dave takes forever to get ready. I figure he'd be a few minutes in the bathroom cleaning up to go out. We're just going to a diner, not the Willard for tea. The good people at the Smith won't flinch at the sight of two queers who look ragged and a little worse for wear. My mom has no patience, and this fruit didn't fall far from the tree. Right as I decide I'm not waiting anymore, my hunger driving me to extreme measures, Dave saunters out of the bathroom. More upsetting is what little improvement all that time and water did for his face or overall appearance. He gets a pass this time, the events of the evening and morning considered.

Regular coffee and heavy food help bring me closer to earth, but my head still spins. For a few moments before the waiter brings out the food, I think I'm going to be sick, but it · subsides and I devour everything I order right when it hits the table. I'm too busy scarfing food down to notice the dainty meal Dave orders and nibbles. He finishes well before I do and discreetly orders a round of mimosas for us. They arrive right when I'm done with my last bite, just in time to make a toast. Dave toasts to a great night last night and as my glass clinks against his, I mention not remembering. A good time was had by all, he insists before offering another toast to tonight, and to the hopes of it being twice as fun.

What Dave lacks in handsomeness, he more than makes up for with an overly polite but endearing grace. Then flashes of his naked body light up my labored brain in bursts. The near-perfect shape of his ample ass, his dancer's body, so lithe and providing. Lost in the lustful thoughts that slash through the prevalent throb of my hangover, I miss him paying the check. He either reads my thoughts or correctly translates my shifty stare and squirming in my chair for the excitement stirring uncomfortably in my pants. Relief can be found around the corner, in his apartment. I left some things there I need to take home.

Back at his place, I quickly collect the few things: my cum stained t-shirt, underwear, keys. No goodbyes necessary. Words can't be spoken when another man's mouth is pressed against mine, his tongue inhibiting mine to that point where I don't even want to talk but taste him once again. My eyes stay closed whenever my face is close to his and our mouths make their extraordinary attempts to consume one another whole. I can't get enough of Dave's supple and accommodating body that contorts to inventive forms in acceptance of whatever I offer. Any hesitancy about coming back tonight to see him again leaves me during the last crucial moments of sex. It will be my pleasure to come again.

The immensity of my headache I expected to vanish with a round of good sex, but it still lingers. For a moment, I forego any suspicions about being drugged and accept Dave's offer to make me a drink. I tell him how sexy it will be to have him make it naked. He agrees and summons me to follow. A fresh pot of coffee is prepared, and our cups are again spiked with a creamy whiskey liqueur. With him naked and my chin resting on his shoulder watching our caffeine countered by more of the hair from the proverbial dog, I take comfort knowing the only poison in there is alcohol. All I really want to do is sleep, and my foolish mention of this prompts an invite to nap with him. I decline, confessing that I need nothing more than to sleep in my own bed after a long, hot shower in my own bathroom.

Did I already apologize for passing out at his place after waking up? I don't ask but offer another one, just in case, and follow up with assurance that blacking out at a stranger's apartment isn't a common occurrence. Last night was only the second time in twenty-plus years of drinking, I reassure him. He passes the test and misses the trap I tried to lay for him. Not once during my apology and horror at my behavior did Dave ever flinch or show any guilt. He's either innocent of drugging me, or a really good actor.

Even as I get ready to finally head home, I can't shake the feeling it's the latter. Sincerity can appear genuine to a mind clouded by hard liquor and little sleep. Our attempt to exchange numbers pulls my attention from his performance to my dead phone battery. Ours aren't the same so his charger is useless to me, and he becomes dismayed that he now can't talk to me on my way home. I still give him my number and tell him to message me his number in return.

All will be better when I get home. I'll recharge, just like my phone. And tonight, a good time on another cold night promises to reunite us for more fun, but with fewer drinks. All this reassuring wears me out enough that I fall asleep on the metro, nearly missing my stop. How do I still feel drunk? My nap on the train subdued the heaviness of it all into a manageable buzz, tolerable only because it just sticks around. The nap I need now must get rid of whatever's left of this hangover. With all the expectations riding on however long I sleep, I say a half-hearted prayer to any god or goddess listening that my anxiety doesn't keep me awake when all I want to do is pass out.

Quick math tells me I slept over three hours, much longer than expected. There's a bunch of messages on my phone. Probably my friends with apologies or questions about what happened after they abandoned me. They can wait. I still have a dull ache at the base of my skull. I decide against trying another drink when my stomach grumbles its request for something more nourishing and substantial. Water assumes the role of sole beverage for a while.

For the first several minutes after waking up, Dave never crosses my mind. But the thought of food reminds me of our breakfast at the diner. Interesting how it takes a trigger to make me remember the guy I had just been with hours earlier. I'm okay with this. Right now, I have other things I'd rather think about, or not think about, considering my head still hurts a little. More food helps. My mind shifts between forced bouts of silence and a flutter of thoughts. Silence seems less interesting to an overactive imagination so in the end it loses.

I ignore the flashing phone while I eat a late lunch. Focus doesn't come easy. Filling my belly assumes any available concentration. Besides, once I look at my phone, I belong to whoever messages me. Goddamn! There are a lot of messages. Only a couple from my people the evening started with but a lot from the person it ended with, at least I'm guessing the unrecognized number that blew up my phone belongs to Dave. And I'm correct. I scan the messages, all variations on *Hope you get home okay — Did you get home okay? — Hope you sleep if you can — Did you get any sleep?* This leads me to a question of my own: *Why did I put my dick in this guy?* I don't want to get into it because I can't remember, and I don't want to start thinking about all the other things I can't remember about last night. Though I did have sex with him again twice this morning. Another question for myself before I have to move on: *How did your heart let sex happen if the fancy wasn't there?* Wearing my heart on my sleeve for sex with strangers isn't my style.

I message a couple friends from last night's group only to wait forever before receiving an answer. Information comes across to clear up what happened until I left with Dave. Everybody was dancing, drinking, screaming conversation over the loud music, having a gay old time. Then some weirdo came over and wouldn't leave, insisting he wanted to buy me a drink and talk. Tired of the guy's insistence, my friends pushed me at him and said they'd be over to get me in about twenty minutes. Then thirty minutes later, everyone split up in separate search parties, but never finding me. My friend is pissed and lectures me about how important it is to leave with whoever you show up with, especially when one of the guys in the group came along just to meet me and go home with me after the bars closed. My protestations mean nothing to my friend. He won't believe me, no matter what I say, so I stop. He doesn't. He speculates why I'd go home with such an ugly, pushy asshole when a much hotter and nicer guy specifically came out to see me. Did I know this beforehand? I inquire. He insists so and I can't argue. None of what he recounts registers as ever happening. I do know that I wouldn't do a friend wrong like that, especially if I knew someone was interested in me. Which now makes me speculate once more exactly how much I had to drink. My asking about anything going on tonight is met with plans that sound amazing. Plans I'm not a part of, it's quickly noted. Besides, the one guy has no interest in me anymore. My friend fucked him last night and will be doing so again tonight.

You snooze, you lose. I have no memory of what the guy looks like, so I guess the loss is minimal. I remember Dave's face and my own forms a foul scowl, like I just tasted a drop of lemon juice. But then I consider his body and how it bends to offer a full-body pleasure I haven't felt in a while – instant arousal. And right on cue a message from him vibrates my phone asking if I still plan to come over.

Red flags wave in my head while I blow dry my hair, fresh out of the shower. I overlook his butterface…the boy can fuck! His pushiness for another date can be construed as flattering, I just need to look at the situation sideways. And to be fair, I drank a lot last night. On top of a full joint on my way to the first bar to meet the guys. That's always been a grave combination for me. No doubt a complete fool stares back at me from the mirror as I scrutinize the details of my haphazardly assembled presentation. The look says easy: jeans, tight white t-shirt, and black combat boots. Easy on, easy off. An easy revenge against my bastard friends – at least tomorrow, I too can brag about having fantastic, body-buzzing, and toe-curling sex. My heart is petty and hard.

Texts blow up my phone the entire way to Dave's and I don't respond until he calls. I send the next call to voicemail and text him back with my ETA. The familiarity of his neighborhood comes back to me the closer I get to his place. Dusk changes the scenery slightly but I've been to this neighborhood before, so I chalk any real recognition up to that. Pretty sure I fucked another guy around these parts. Very distinguishable is Dave, standing at the door with a smile and a welcoming hug. He tells me he's happy to see me and I return the sentiment. It's not a total lie. If my heart wasn't in it, I'd be someplace else.

He ushers me upstairs and makes annoying double-entendres from the elevator all the way into his apartment. I see where he wants this to go, and I am genuinely confused because I thought I made it clear earlier how hungry I am. He convinces me to have one drink at least before we leave to eat. For him it becomes an excuse to make out with me. "If this keeps up, I'm gonna start eating your face," I tell him. My lame joke works as perfect interference. When we get up to leave, I realize I never took a single sip of my drink. He pours it down the sink with a smile right before we walk out the door.

The double-entendres continue to the restaurant, during dinner, and even still as we head back to his place. He almost succeeds in killing the mood but I'm horny and on a mission so we're going to soldier through to make it happen. Does Dave talk like this so people will overlook his face and focus on the promises he makes with his body? Still, the evening sorely lacks better conversation. My best efforts to steer it away from sexual innuendo all fail. I swear if he makes one more comment about the light meal he deliberately ate at dinner, I'll walk away. It never comes so that means now we both will, too. Happily, I'd like to add.

Another drink replaces the old one I never touched a minute after we walk into his living room. I thank him but decline. Dave looks confused, hurt almost, down to the exaggeration of a pouting bottom lip. I defend myself by admitting that I won't be able to stop with just one. He amps up his insistence. I decline again because I can't handle another drunken night like the one before. He claims to understand but now keeps up a wounded act that annoys me more than the suggestive double speak from earlier. I decide we should just fuck before I lose more nerve and interest. Nothing about tonight resembles what I saw in my head. Not really sure what I expected but my patience with Dave started to wear thin before I left my own apartment. One thing I know lies in store, and that's good sex, so I instigate this by kissing him. I keep my eyes closed so the sight of his face that close to my own doesn't distract me or kill my erection. Without the blur of alcohol, Dave's face and previous demeanor aggravate my sensibilities. Fortunately, he likes a little rough play so my hand over his mouth excites him. I start to think whether or not a beard might help his face a bit. But then even his moans find a way to grate my nerves. I've barely put my dick in him and already he's carrying on like I've been wearing him out for hours with a cock twice my size. Chants of "fuck me daddy!" pound in my head until I finally excuse myself for a moment. At the bar I pour my own drink, to be safe, and from a glass near the back of the stacks, just to be extra sure. The sweet intoxication of liquor needs to work its magic fast, so I take another shot. Then another.

Too many drinks and my performance begins to suffer. The two sides of the scale finally tip in favor of drunkenness giving way to disappointment instead of pleasure. Well, according to Dave's point of view. Am I disappointed? Sure. But a peculiar pleasure comes from disappointing him. I would've loved to have had sex with Dave again, his body so accommodating to how I like to fuck. The positions that boy can twist his body into and how he takes a pounding is next level. But something was missing from before. Dave needs help becoming tolerable. Maybe instead of drinking so much myself I should've just made Dave get drunk. But then he might have passed out and either way our night together would end without orgasm. Once he realizes my limp penis cannot be revived, he walks to the bar and downs what's left of the same bottle of scotch I made my own drinks from. He wants to catch up, that way we can just sit and chat. And cuddle. Christ that sounds insufferable which Dave proves soon enough after we get dressed. We have trouble getting beyond painful small talk. Pauses in both our banter bring on a case of the nods as our heads take turns drooping, simultaneous and hilarious. Until I win and keep my eyes open and head up the longest. "Lightweight," I taunt under my breath, so I don't wake him. Waiting a few minutes for complete assurance that Dave is passed out, I finally feel comfortable enough to get up and leave. I swipe a bottle of water on my way out to help flood my blood.

The fresh air and walk clear my head and I wish for another bottle of water. Thank god for random street vendors. Two bucks later, another bottle washes free more poison from my system. But being drunk makes me want to be even more drunk. The awareness of how fucked-up that craving sounds hits hard inside an already tortured skull. My sudden cognizance of approaching loneliness makes me crave the company of someone, anyone really. The feel of another person's skin, mouth, insides…desire reminds me I never finished earlier. Blue balls need relief. I smile realizing that boring Dave and his shitty face, and not me being shitfaced, killed the previous urge – stiff proof now presses uncomfortably inside my jeans. Complete satisfaction overwhelms me knowing that all of these essentials I crave can be obtained with relative ease at the same place. I also now realize I've become that parody of a faggot who only knows how to solve a problem with more of the same problem. Scratch a wound until the scab opens up. Keep going so it never has a chance to heal. You only live once, they say, so why not bleed out when life is still interesting, and enough youth remains to enjoy it? To hell with all these deep thoughts. I want to feel alive and not think my life away. I want to bleed. I wonder what bar my friends are at right now.

ABLE BODIES

CONSEQUENCES CAME fast. Gossip progressed, pregnant with the promise of becoming myth. With most of the town unsure of exactly what transpired, and given the nature of the act, all parties agreed that such a hasty departure amidst the swirl of rumors and unanswered questions seemed damning. The Pastor possessed a sterling reputation, completely without fault. Some felt sad to see him go. The mother of the boy who drowned didn't want him to go. She instead wanted him dead, swamp-buried in an unmarked grave.

Luann Owens, with no middle name, knew no other home but the same small town and four walls that contained her dreams and confined her life. With her son dead, hearsay about paternity would start again so Luann took action, the truth a promised delivery. Nobody thought the answer dared carry its message of hatred and destruction up into the sky as a pillar of black, acrid smoke. But poor Luann, alone with no reason to live, suffered enough, subsisted enough. Men of God and men in general were born to make empty promises for services and championed causes. For her, one accomplishment offered both redemption and reward in one swift flick.

Sleepy, rural, southern towns offered little by way of stimulation, so that day's repercussions caused hurricane winds to turbulently spin the gossip mill. "The tragedy," as it came to be known, happened right before the Honeybee Festival, the annual highlight that inaugurated the onset of autumn. So much of the year passed, humdrum, with perpetual warmth. Days congregated into anthologies of dull experiences. One resembled the other with the shared calamity of stagnation. Any year bled into the next until the stream of life flowed by and out of a person, who realized too late all the time spent. Everybody knew everyone else. People's business became common knowledge and bartered. No action escaped the scrutiny of the denizens from Hahira, Georgia. That year, Elvis confessed in code that he was the Devil in disguise and not you. Everyone prayed for a miracle which came true: that big phony never had a number one hit again.

Within a year of his arrival, Pastor Samuel Park ingratiated himself to the entirety of his new congregation, incredible for a town full of people slow to change. Youth still animated his motives at the age of thirty-two and with that came the credibility his message needed in order to be successful. The Philippians 3:21 underscored his message: *Who shall change our vile body, that it may be fashioned like unto his glorious body, according to the working whereby he is able even to subdue all things unto himself.*

"The young can do anything they set their trained minds to do," the Pastor said from the pulpit with utmost conviction, "and from their able bodies can come whatever their minds imagine." The message stirred and inspired the assembly.

Belief regenerated, stronger than ever in young and old alike. Elders thought comfortably about leaving their legacy in the hands of an unproven generation, moved by the young Pastor from a faraway county up north closer to Atlanta. Beyond the last place he lived, his age and his credentials, little information found its way to the citizens of Hahira. His endless charisma poured out in a gentle baritone that promised respect and trust as rewards. Feelings of purpose gripped others in the community, all radiating outward from the center of the church and the good Pastor. The pews swelled until even the nonbelievers benefitted from the good words and deeds of Pastor Park.

Something akin to wonder stimulated young Patrick Owens when he watched the Pastor command the congregation from behind the pulpit. He felt the sway of promises and the influence of the man inspiring him to improve. Words replete with the power to uplift or condemn at any second aroused an unplumbed fervor in the young boy. No more berating himself for a lack of purpose. A clearer path to his future presented itself in Pastor Park and the lesson he held so dear.

"Absolutely not," Luann started when Patrick flippantly mentioned the possibility of becoming a Pastor himself, "it's limiting." She corrected her tone, removing contempt. "Worse than limiting," she continued, "that work might keep you here or trapped in some other small town just like this one. Be a man of God, that's fine. But it would be more satisfying when the money you make is earned through the efforts of an honest day's work and not just expected to magically appear every Sunday morning."

A young, unmarried man of the cloth became popular in small towns. The hope of marriage a boon to the single women of Lowndes County and the other counties connected. Luann Owens never counted herself among the possible contestants. Her sole purpose in life was the proper raising of her son. The condescending pity of the first Pastor she served gave her a job at seventeen, a purpose. Swollen duties matched the action in her belly. The soldier's who she loved before he left for war?

The insidious pastor who usurped her autonomy? The story became a kinder, more acceptable version she promoted even to her son: Patrick's father became the brave soldier who died in a war. Either way, Luann suffered through an unsolicited life of service. This evolved over time into the lighthearted anecdote that she "came with the church" whenever one Pastor retired, and another assumed the reins. By then, the jurisdiction of her duties extended only to internal, domestic upkeep. With a new, younger pastor living in the house, the bulk of her work for the first few months consisted of washing then returning a steady collection of neighborly dishes intended as special offering plates for the Pastor's favors.

"What could she have to offer?" tongues wagged when the Pastor's deteriorating house began to demand more of Luann's time.

The reinforced Patrick found himself caught off guard when questioned by the Pastor's throng of imperious and ruthless would-be suitors. He didn't know the answers nor did he completely understand the intentions of his interrogators. To his knowledge, nothing more than friendly banter during working hours was ever exchanged. No secretive glances or coded innuendo during the handful of times Pastor Park visited their house for supper. Yet the hissing tones of jealousy shaded the voices of these venomous women, making the boy leery of their prying. "What business is it of yours, may I ask?" became the emboldened Patrick's subsequent response. The posing of a question in response to another question only fanned the flames of gossip.

All the chin wagging found its way to Patrick by way of his only friend, Marylynn Washington. Information about his mama and the Pastor affected the invented future with her friend. These two notorious adults would be her in-laws. After all, she and Patrick were to be married. Or so only she believed. The single reason for her curiosity – she had a right to know. The evidence would be hers and hers alone. Why share anything with a town of people who called her and her own mama trash? She insisted her rights be recognized, she said out loud one day. Patrick thought otherwise and had no problem telling her so. He held Marylynn's heart gripped tight enough to give them both fear of any sudden, disruptive motions. One wrong move from her and Patrick could rip out the still-beating organ. Persistence meant eventual success. Finally, she wore him down enough to talk.

"I can't believe you've had a key this whole time and you never told me," Marylynn stated one afternoon, an edge of anger cutting through.

"There's a lot I never told you," Patrick replied in his usual matter of fact manner.

"Like stuff about your mama and the Pastor?" she said. The bitter blade of jealousy sliced at but missed its intended target. Patrick remained focused and dismissive. All that mattered then and there was proving Marylynn wrong, and from her, the rest of Hahira would know there was nothing wrong going on between his mama and Pastor Park.

Marylynn's refused to give up belief in an affair. She was satisfied, in part, since zero proof meant no victory for either side. Patrick wasn't satisfied at all.

"Look around since you probably still don't believe me. But don't touch anything and be careful. Someone might be here."

That prospect appealed to Marylynn and lit up her resolute face with a mischievous smirk.

"I'll look upstairs, you look down here." These were Patrick's instructions.

Before he turned to creep up the staircase, Marylynn was gone in a flash. Patrick rolled his eyes and went upstairs. Silence prevailed around the entire second floor until he heard a low hissing, the closer he got to the back of the long hall, near the bathroom. The other rooms held no mystery, he remained fixated only on the low noise. Each step closer made his temperature rise and humidity greeted him upon reaching the end of the hall.

The bathroom door was open about five inches and offered just enough space to peer inside. In spite of the electric switch turned off, enough light was available to show Patrick the source of noise and mugginess. Pastor Park was in the shower, oblivious to anybody else in the parsonage. The simple act of taking a shower, the machine-like movements of cleanliness, became something else for Patrick. Large hands seemed to control the water that streamed down the Pastor's body. Soaked, dark fur clung to his chest, arms and legs. All of him was made erotic with waves of his hands that gave a hardness to whatever part of his body they encountered. Muscles bulged and remained stiff. It was only a matter of seconds before those inspirational, miraculous hands found their way between his legs and lent a generous stiffness to his sex.

Patrick imagined those hands on his body, his own limbs and muscles tight from nerves and excitement. And then the fantasy hands grabbed the length of Patrick's own sex, which made it harder than he had ever known. Sweat instead of shower water wet his brow, that part had no correlation to the previous, brief fancy. An uncomfortable tightness in the front of his pants drew immediate attention to the one thing that carried over from the daydream. A quick adjustment almost allowed Patrick the comfort to fall back into the fantasy, but his name being whispered from downstairs kept him from slipping. A final glance at Pastor Park's soaked body warmed by steam and shower stream was an impromptu parting gift.

"Nobody upstairs?" Marylynn asked.

"The Pastor, but he was alone."

"How do you know? Did you see him?"

"Yeah…" Patrick admitted, even to his own astonishment. The lie he had in store was wasted.

"Oh. Okay. Well, I guess that *is* proof. This would be the best time of day to be carrying on in secret."

Patrick's thinking lingered on the offered truth about seeing the Pastor. When no further criticism about Pastor Park or his mama was offered, the focus of his attention was how easy Marylynn dropped the subject. But then he saw why, or rather, who made her stop talking all together.

The tight weave of gray fabric is what Patrick focused on first. A quick shift in the stranger's stance drew Patrick's attention to the immaculate two-toned, black and white shoes. The feet that carried the man seemed too small for the task. Then Patrick fully sized up the stranger, who carried with him the faint smell of something sulfurous. Over six feet tall, he towered over the other two, sizing the both of them in turn. Lanky limbs belied the muscles that instructed each graceful movement; the removal of his hat by a bony hand at the end of an impossibly long arm, the crooked bow he gave in greeting, and then almost the precise motions again, but in reverse.

"Hey. How're y'all?" The words drew out into a long wave

of slurred syllables. They were the only thing slow about the man who the longer he looked at Patrick and Marylynn, the more they began to fear anything he might do next. Walking circles around them like a vulture spiraling inward upon carrion, staring mostly at Patrick, he spoke again. The words made the quarry wince. "Pastor home?" A hissing lisp imbued the question with a hint of danger.

"No." Patrick spat out, cutting off Marylynn. "We're just leaving after cleaning the place up a bit."

"Hmm. Well, who are you, boy?" The words ran together as they slipped from his lips. The drawl and timbre of his voice was unlike anything Patrick had ever heard. Almost otherworldly, some menace made the words and sentences uncomfortable.

"My name is Patrick. My mama works here."

"Ah, right. So you're Luann's boy...well, well..."

The man in the gray suit circled Patrick again, ignoring Marylynn altogether. Only when the man stopped less than two feet from his face did Patrick notice that the knot of the purple tie around his neck was off center, just to the left of his Adam's apple. A ruby clip held the silk tie to his shirt and it glinted in the sun whenever the man spoke.

"When you see Pastor Park, tell him I'll be by tomorrow on my way home since I seem to have missed him today."

"And who should I tell him came calling?"

"He knows my name. I reckon you know my name too, boy, you're just too goddamn afraid to say it." The red ruby bounced like a red-hot fire ball while his chest raised and fell during his light laughter. "See you later." It sounded like a warning.

Patrick and Marylynn stood upright and frozen until the man in the gray suit and hat went completely out of sight. Even after the man was gone, neither really knew what to say. Soon enough, Patrick broke silence with a sharp intake of air. The exhale was louder and after his lungs again filled with air, he asked a question.

"Did you think something was wrong with that man?"

"Yeah. He barely looked at me."

Marylynn's burgeoning vanity was lost on Patrick, especially when the latter was focused with something else on his mind.

"Did he seem *evil* to you?"

"Bad, wicked, so sure, why not evil. Is that why you lied and said Pastor Park wasn't home?"

"Yeah. I wanted to protect him."

Marylynn's response was a sideways glance and an uninterested nod. She could be just as disinterested when whatever she offered wasn't accepted. And even when his mind was somewhere else, Patrick maintained his presence in the space around him and could read the room, so to speak.

"I'm going to tell Pastor about him. I understand if you got other things to do…" Patrick remarked.

"I do. I'll catch up with you later. Want me to come by around four?" Marylynn asked for reassurance.

"Should be fine. See ya then."

Patrick was halfway inside the parsonage before the final word and without waiting for any reply, he closed the door and locked both locks. The noisy click of the final bolt lock alerted the Pastor that someone had entered. Patrick's voice calling out his name gave Pastor Park cause to relax when the identity of the intruder was known.

"Upstairs!" Pastor Park bellowed from above, but Patrick was already ascending the staircase.

He reached the bathroom in a state of panic. The Pastor stood, waiting, facing the door. The ready words of warning were stifled by the Pastor's greeting. Only in tight white briefs, skin still damp and red from a scalding shower, the image and reception took Patrick's breath away. No wind left meant the words still laid in wait.

Patrick's eyes roamed and devoured the full extent of Pastor Park's body. Dark fur clung to parts of his chest, arms and legs. Wet or dry, hair covered most of his body, its dark color a sharp contrast to his pale skin. The cruel Georgia sun only ever met his face, neck and hands, the rest kept covered by his unofficial uniform of dress slacks and a long sleeve shirt never allowed a casual moment during its service. So, for Patrick to see him stripped of everything but his underwear was a miracle. The glimpse earlier no longer mattered to Patrick. That opportunity was stolen, this one was granted.

"Are you okay?" the Pastor asked with concern.

Words still refused to help Patrick explain anything. He had been reduced to a watchtower.

Pastor Park approached the statue-like youth. "Patrick? What's the matter? You look like you've seen a ghost." He placed his hand on the boy's shoulder.

Worse! I think I just saw a devil! The thought never made the transition to statement of fact. But the Pastor's touch on his arm made it stiffen and again Patrick thought back to the earlier peek. So far only an arm. The hope of being touched more graduated to a wish. Patrick's saucer-wide blue eyes watched as the Pastor's free hand reached and cupped the back of his neck and pulled him closer. Clean breath asked the next question mere inches away from Patrick's dumbfounded face.

"Patrick? What's wrong? Talk to me. No cats in here to get your tongue so spit it out."

Warm skin burned Patrick through the outside barrier of his clothing, the only thing physical separating him and the Pastor. With the heat came a compelling magnetism that wanted anything within a certain proximity to come alive. Patrick felt its pull but so little space already existed between them. Before the action registered and gave him time to object, Patrick's body lost its resistance and pressed against the Pastor. Shoulders met shoulders, hips joined hips and still unhindered by rational thinking, their mouths met last. The shocking realization of what was taking place scared Patrick. His eyes opened with the expectation of seeing an angered man glaring back, his own eyes full of hate. Instead, Patrick saw the Pastor's eyes shut tight. Nothing indicated distress. The only concern belonged to Patrick.

Everything he ever heard about what he was doing came from hateful mouths predicting horrible outcomes. If no good ever came from it, why did it feel natural to Patrick? Kissing a man made more sense as a sensual outlet than doing the same thing with a girl. But men still weren't supposed to kiss men.

The Pastor wrapped his arms around Patrick and eliminated what space remained between them. Any resistance became Patrick's alone. Never during the torrent of doubt and questions rushing through the confused boy's mind did Pastor Park interrupt the kiss or try to separate. His actions were backed by a mature assurance. Roaming hands knew when to venture, where and just how far. Patrick responded perfectly and in kind. Even when the Pastor led him across the hall into the bedroom, already dimly lit, seemingly already prepared for a carnal encounter. What amazed and excited Patrick the most was just what their bodies were able to do and endure.

Afterwards, Patrick stared at the Pastor, whose own gaze stayed fixed on the ceiling. A tide of questions with answers and consequences beyond his youthful understanding ebbed and flowed. For the time being, feeling the still warm body of the naked Pastor so close to him subdued bad judgments. Before words escaped his still tingling lips, Pastor Park turned to look at the boy in his bed. His smile again prevented Patrick from muttering anything. With a kiss, the Pastor made sure those words stayed down and he kept them suppressed with more flesh and promises. And those kisses offered Patrick his first glimpse into what could be beautiful about love.

The days that followed saw Patrick as more of a presence around the parsonage. Luann didn't mind since extra hands were helpful with tasks better suited for a teenage boy and not idle for the devil to use. This new cooperation made her feel closer to a son she would hopefully lose to college then the wide world in two years when he graduated high school. Those were the beginnings of her expectations and since spending more time with him, she began to think they were shared goals. If not, then the communal extra time could be used to persuade him otherwise. Pastor Park was sure to share her wishes for the boy's future. He assured them both separately and individually that he did.

Pride swelled Patrick's chest. Under the Pastor's careful tutelage and instruction, the boy's muscles became harder, while his mind grew sharper. Any attempt to debate or reason revealed a shrewd mind at work with little chance of changing it. Often, truths were his alone, their understanding personal and known to nobody else. These perceptions then fostered a new path directed by an ever-evolving moral compass. His understanding gave him insight, along with unpredictability. But the arrogance had yet to become dangerous. The boy was still in the throes of adolescence, cocky posturing was expected and only discouraged if someone could get hurt.

For however much Patrick was sure of his favored position among the other able-bodied boys, there hid a fear of losing favor, of having to share any devotion. Access to the parsonage by way of his mama was how he made sure, using her and his very own key to hush any suspicions when they arose. With no one to think anything other than Pastor Park instructing Patrick in the ways of body, mind and soul, within a month their relationship flourished. The Pastor, training his astute student, passed on knowledge and experience. Patrick became the bottomless font for whatever flowed from his teacher.

A newfound sense of individuality was difficult for a boy of sixteen to carry and it showed in the exaggerated swagger that was more imitation than anything authentic. The taste he had only made him want more liberation, which he took to mean it was already his. Presumed liberties extended to Patrick's attitudes towards his peers. The shy, demure boy thought himself an adult, finally the man of the house which was his to inherit. But he and Luann were hardly at their own house anymore, especially together and at night. The real man of that house was tender, loving to a fault, and firm in his belief that Patrick's journey along the path to manhood with able body, mind and soul had only just begun. Also, Pastor Park reminded him, everyone's passage is personal, only striving to better themselves and not best others. But having the Pastor's preference and sharing his bed told Patrick that he was indeed special, therefore he had to exceed. Patrick couldn't think of anything contrary to the belief so it stuck.

When arrogance and ego failed to inflate his head, they began to manifest in unsettling ways. The first was certainly a thought he believed he could never have, but there it was, with many more to come. And the way this idea came to Patrick was during a typical Sunday service. Everything about it was customary: the rising number of attendees, the length of the sermon, even the gossip of jealous soon-to-be spinsters still angry and accusatory of plain old Luann catching the Pastor's eye. Patrick couldn't help but grin. *If only these dumb women knew,* he thought under his smirking. So much would go wrong. Infinitely more harm than good, should anybody ever know. The power of keeping a secret like that was more beneficial than Patrick knew in the beginning.

Luann went on with business as usual, none the wiser of her son's entanglement. All she saw were Patrick's physical and mental improvements. With any luck, Luann believed, the Pastor would fashion her son in his image and make of Patrick the man she began to see in a different, prospective light.

Transforming from a shy, inward boy into a sure and solid young man flabbergasted nobody more than Patrick. Still, beneath the façade and over emphasized, straight as a board posture, was a childlike soul that at any moment, from any insult or attack on his defenses, would collapse inward again. The sensitive slouch would return, and his eyes wouldn't see much beyond his shoes. Or so he thought.

The habit of stopping by unannounced was outright discouraged by Pastor Park. Yet the most able of his bodies never listened. What's the point of privilege if it can't be used to your advantage? Patrick would respond. The petulance of the boy's reply startled the Pastor and the first time it was used as an excuse became the beginning of mistrust and then concern. Patrick was harmless. Infatuated, but not dangerous. A smarter man might have figured out a way to ward off any unplanned intrusion, at the very least a string of bells around the doorknob that jingled whenever opened or closed.

The interior of the house stood still with an uncommon silence for that time of day. Noontime meant the Pastor was either at his desk working on sermons or in the kitchen in some stage of lunch. All of this took place downstairs. Pastor Park's beat up Ford was outside which indicated he was almost certain to be home. Curious, but not worrisome. Waiting became the decision of what to do next.

Flopping on the couch the precise moment a noise groaned from somewhere in the house might have made it go unnoticed had it not been for another less than a minute later. The structure was too old to settle any more but the right age to start falling apart. Not until a third more guttural human noise came from some place more definitive did Patrick change his mind. Maybe someone was home. Maybe the Pastor was in trouble.

Fear kept Patrick's gait up the stairs cautious and calculated. Not knowing what he might find, or even who, scared him and regret grew with each step upstairs. The closer he got to the noise, the more the noise came to resemble grunts. The end of the hall resonated with the sound once Patrick reached the top of the stairs and rounded the corner to his left. What frightened him the most was the awareness of two voices combining to make the din worse. Curiosity lost paradise, Pastor Park taught his congregation, but Patrick felt his concern was more important. But trepidation also colored that decision and each stride forward instilled a new sense of dread.

Instead of an immediate reveal, a half-closed door kept the source obscured, just in time for Patrick to take a deep breath and get the gumption to finally look. Another minute would pass before he had the nerve to peek through the crack, careful not to touch the door or be seen in return.

A monster with multiple limbs thrashing wildly transformed into its true form once Patrick's eyes adjusted to the room's curtained and dim interior. Distinct shapes of arms and legs became clear, even if who was doing what was still elusive. Hands that held feet let go and fell forward around a throat. Those freed feet and legs wrapped around the physical aggressor, refusing release. Rhythmic buttocks drove grinding hips into the other's body. A throttled moan escaped the man on the bottom. Though distorted by muffling gestures, the voice sounded familiar to Patrick. Another longer, deeper growl confirmed the identity. A hideous and hissed "yes" was an acceptance of approval with the final constant drawn out longer than necessary.

The chill that ran through Patrick's entire being froze him to the spot, forcing him to continue the detestable vigil. Movement on the bed mocked the boy's static, cemented stance. The shifting of positions put the offensive physiques in better view. Who once was underneath pushed the intruding, lanky body backwards before straddling it and writhing with its own impressive assault. Arms held aloft and straight forward, propped under knees bent from squatting, were the same arms that embraced Patrick in that same room. Now they were incapable of much besides keeping balance. The Pastor's face never fully came into view since it tilted up to stare at the ceiling. The man on his back let his head fall over the edge of the bed, exposing the face of the Devil.

Shrill laughter forced Patrick to shiver free from his paralysis. "Yes, boy!" the Devil shrieked over and over. Those two words were the Pastor's favorites when he stared into Patrick's eyes, deep inside. They became blasphemous and tarnished in the mouth of this evil. And the act of sex was only supposed to be shared between Patrick and the Pastor. Another sacred performance made profane by the malevolent man fucking Pastor Park.

The image seared itself into Patrick's mind long after he left the house. At first, he barely realized he was outside, stunned and forgetful of his flight down the stairs, away from the Pastor in bed with an abomination. By the time he got home, a couple hours had passed. That trip was also a blur. Jumbled thoughts joined shifting southern scenes of pine trees and heat rising off blacktop, waves from strangers and swarms of pesky insects. His mind and opinions changed faster than the gentle shifts between South Georgia seasons. One thing was certain and became an all-encompassing obsession since Patrick could focus on nothing else until every last bit of affection and respect he held for Pastor Park was squeezed out, leaving a dry and useless husk of a heart.

The difference in his demeanor became evident the very next day. An appointment with the pastor overlooked for the sake of staying away came with an immediate visit from the man himself. "It's not like him to miss out on plans with you, of all people," Luann stated, sure of a logical explanation. Pride beamed from her face at the thought of how special her son was to the Pastor, and then again to her own closeness and privileges. She walked the Pastor to Patrick's room and knocked. In the Owens house, no response meant enter.

Patrick sat on his bed dressed only in his underwear. Luann turned and hid her face in embarrassment. "Why didn't you say you weren't decent?" Patrick offered no sound or movement as a reaction. He didn't even blink. "Well anyway," she continued, but with her stare fixed opposite her near-naked son, "you're late for whatever you had planned with Pastor Park at his house so he's here now." Then, to the Pastor, "He's all yours."

"Thank you, Luann," he returned. When she could no longer be seen from the entryway to Patrick's room, he closed the door then locked it.

"Is everything okay, Patrick?" Pastor Park asked simply enough. His voice carried a gentle concern. At this Patrick made the first slight motion by raising his eyes and setting them on the Pastor. But that was all. No explanation, least of all. Pastor Park asked the question a second time. With that, the boy's contemplation returned to whatever previously held their blank attention. "Talk to me, Patrick. You're not yourself—"

The suddenness of Patrick's flinching, as if rudely awakened, startled the Pastor. Patrick obviously had something he wanted to say but the reasons he didn't remained his own.

"You can talk to me. You can tell me anything."

The young eyes that glared out at Pastor Park did so behind fresh, streaming tears. The Pastor sat on the bed next to the boy and offered an awkward embrace, courtesy of the slouched position and reticence of its recipient. Immediately upon feeling the Pastor's embrace, Patrick shifted and sat upright to better accommodate the strong arms that held him tight. More tears erupted while convulsions heaved the young boy's body. Once their intensity diminished, Pastor Park broke the embrace and pulled his face away but just a few inches from Patrick's own. The Pastor's next intended offering was the tenderness of a soft, understanding kiss. With unexpected force, Patrick shoved Pastor Park away, almost completely off the bed.

Collecting himself, the Pastor again asked his initial question, followed once more by the reassurance that Patrick could confide in him. Pastor Park was not expecting a response in the form of a question.

"You know you can tell me anything too, right?" The mocking tone of the return made the Pastor uneasy. A sneer formed at the corners of Patrick's tightly sealed mouth. Even that subtle betrayal of what tormented him inside upset him with what little it revealed. Before the Pastor could reply, Patrick cut him off with two words that needed no further explanation or even a request for one. The certitude of their delivery, despite the hushed and polite tone that projected them, existed as ample reason to take heed.

"Please leave."

Not even the coaxing of a devoted mother pulled an explanation from her son. Luann could count on one hand the amount of times he spoke to her all day. If nothing needed to be done around the house, he was in his room with the door closed. When Patrick asked if he could take supper to his room, Luann reached her breaking point and demanded an explanation.

"Things are just *different* now..." Patrick offered as haphazard yet cryptic reasoning.

"What does that mean?" she further inquired.

"It just means things are different now."

"How? What?" Luann struggled with controlling her confusion.

"You wouldn't understand. Or even want to."

"Try me." Luann implored.

But Patrick already clammed up, once more dismayed at giving away any clues that might unlock the secret of what changed him overnight from a devoted boy whose able body he dedicated to both god and his servant in Pastor Park to the withdrawn and sulking young man who refused to talk. "May I be excused?" became his final sentence spoken that evening, not even offering his mother a simple "good night" before turning off his light only a few feet away from her open bedroom door.

"Whatever it is that's eating you up isn't going to keep you from work," Luann insisted the next day when Patrick came out of his room undressed and not ready for the day's chores at the parsonage. Her usual gentle demeanor had sharpened to a cutting blade that swiped at his heels to keep him in motion. She only asked one question that morning and the dour response it elicited prevented her from asking any more. With Patrick, Luann resolved that she would not speak unless spoken to, and that was even more scarce than the previous day.

The same treatment was extended to the Pastor. Worse, since Luann noticed Patrick did not utter a single syllable to Pastor Park, nor did he look at him without reason. And never were the two alone together in the same room. Patrick saw to that with diligence. Work that day was performed as if a phantom helper begrudgingly did the bare minimum required for the job.

Luann invited Marylynn for supper that evening. If she couldn't get her son to confess, with hope he might disclose the secret to his friend. Doubt persisted since Patrick wouldn't talk to his best friend the Pastor at all, but relying on more recent confidences of an older friend would at least confirm one suspicion she harbored. Patrick was sore with Pastor Park, she supposed. The result delivered was expected yet exaggerated: Patrick's withdrawal was so complete that he reacted to no outside stimuli, be it a question or concern. The two ladies then spoke among themselves, determined to not let the sour milk of the boy's petulance spoil their dinner. Lively and inviting laughter fell on Patrick's deaf ears and unaffected senses so when he eventually asked to be dismissed, his request was granted with pleasure and no hesitation.

Sleep stayed away just as it had the night before when the wounds of the Pastor's betrayal were still fresh and seeping. So much needed to be digested and processed before Patrick felt a return to normal might be possible. Fear made him believe normalcy didn't belong to him anymore, that he had no right to it after bearing witness to both sides of the Pastor's perversions. Wracked with confusion, he lay motionless all night despite the tumult of thoughts and reactions wrestling inside his head. The reconciliation of who he was and who he wanted to be proved impossible. Defeat waited with any decision proposed. Where he stood, his mother and two friends could not understand him or the war using his brain as its theatre. Maybe one did, but his furtive behavior meant he had been lost for a while. The other two people, the ones closest to him, would surely be lost if they knew any of the damning details. A renewed devotion to his own secrecy would, with hope, prevent any more peeks into his turmoil. Patrick vowed to find a solution, regardless of how long it might take.

Resigning to that providence proved to be the only chance he had for even a few hours of restful sleep.

The work Patrick chose to do at the parsonage required optimum sunlight, so the shorter days were to his liking. Before long, Pastor Park needed yet another hand to pick up the slack. Since her son could not be counted on for much beyond the bare minimum, Luann relented and gave her approval. That is when a new face began to replace Patrick's and a new name was spoken with the pride once reserved for Patrick. His increasing absence left little room for notice or care. Luann took notice and it concerned her. Here was an opportunity being taken away from her son by the very church that stripped her of all promise to lift herself any higher than a glorified servant. An exasperation for that son of hers festered as she watched the hopes Patrick had heaped on his broadened shoulders get shrugged off with such indifference.

An entire week passed, and Patrick never stepped within a hundred-yard radius of the parsonage. Luann was the first to observe, and the only person to know that the words "Pastor Park" or "the Pastor" never came out of his mouth at home. And Patrick's replacement, if referred to at all, had been reduced to "what's his name." Patrick knew his name. The boys had known each other since elementary school as the minimal population of Hahira stipulated. "What's his name" spoke better and got better grades all throughout school. Without a doubt, this added to his injury of bearing witness to Pastor Park's newest indiscretion. An intimate act once thought reserved for him destroyed and further debased by imagined phantasies to trouble his sleep. Beyond being smarter, "what's his name" offered nothing that Patrick felt he didn't have in abundance.

"He has the time to help," Pastor Park explained when Patrick finally built up the gumption to confront the first of many imagined demons alive at the parsonage.

"I'm sure that's all…" Patrick replied. The implication of his tone stopped Pastor Park cold. The boy now had all his attention as the man looked up from the handwritten pages strewn on his desk.

"That *is* all. I don't like what you're implying—"

"And I don't like what you're doing," Patrick interrupted, "or who you're doing it with."

The relief brought on by the minor confession liberated Patrick only a little before the fear of his revelation threatened to scare him back into the comfort of a cage.

"I told you, I'm not doing anything with—" The Pastor was stopped short of saying the forbidden name by Patrick's slammed fist on the hard, wooden desk.

"I'm not talking about him, Pastor…" Boldness erupted from the pit of Patrick's stomach mixed with bile. Pastor Park's smokescreen made him sick enough to finally confess everything.

All he saw that terrible day came spewing out of him along with the wretched emotions that upset him. The repercussions of it all were then heaved on top of an already appalling pile. One barely looked at the other during Patrick's admission for fear of arousing further antagonism. Silence hung heavy in the room when Patrick finished; he regretted the words the instant they left his mouth. Pastor Park did not know what to say, or where to start. More so, he wondered why Patrick needed to know anything about his past at all. An explanation was duly owed but the Pastor still had no idea what to say. When their eyes did meet and lock for more than a moment, their intentions and wants were recognizable. At last, one unexpected action denied everything behind their eyes but still granted an earned relief. Pastor Park stood up and left his own house without saying a single word.

Swift legs then carried Patrick instinctively away from the parsonage and in the direction of a known destination. The only formal directive the sturdy limbs received kept them from taking him home. The Pastor would think to look for him there when he decided the conversation required revisiting. Before he bothered to worry about time, Patrick arrived at a house he'd been to several times, but only once did he ever enter. A single bedroom light meant only one person occupied the shabby structure.

"I don't know why you came here but I'm glad you did." Marylynn proclaimed. Her stance reflected the annoyed attitude she felt for her friend. Her arms crossed, hip jutting to the left, tight lips withheld their assessment until they softened from mixing with spit. "I haven't seen you in a while. Not since supper at your house that one time. You were acting odd then. What's bothering you?"

"Not sure you'd really understand," Patrick answered. "Besides, I'm not sure exactly what I should or shouldn't tell you."

"I've known you since we were five. If you can't trust me, who can you trust?"

With nowhere else to go, Patrick ended up at Marylynn's house. The first and only other time he saw the interior of the house, her mom chased him out with a broom. Completing the scene was the crazy lady screaming at her daughter for bringing a boy home like a little whore at seven. *Dirty little boys only want to see one thing!* Marylynn's drunk mother yelled and before speaking, those words ricocheted around an already bruised brain.

"There's just...too much."

"Start at the beginning, then." When a moment passed without any response from Patrick: "or just start with the smallest problem."

The last request elicited a light chuckle from Patrick. "I don't think none of 'em are small."

The friends shared the discomfort brought on by the dense silence.

"You know what might help?" Marylynn offered, her voice spiked with a tinge of wickedness, "a shot of liquid courage."

"What's that?" Patrick asked with sincere innocence.

"It's what my mama calls whisky."

"Naw. I can't drink that! You know what the Bible says!"

"I do but I also know that what you wanna say ain't gonna come out unless it's liquored out of you. It's the quickest way to get the devil out of you, my mama says."

"Drinking is the quickest way to get the devil in you. Besides, it's not a devil in me I'm scared of—" Patrick stopped with expressing the thought before he fully got started. As a response to Marylynn's intense and piqued curiosity, he instead offered a consolation: "but there is something inside me that scares me awake most nights."

Again, the silence choked like a heavy fog.

"Then we'll start you off with just one shot." And before Patrick offered protest, "Gotta get a worse devil in ya if you wanna get the other devils out. And I'll match whatever you drink, that way we'll go to hell together."

Marylynn took the restored silence as Patrick's acceptance.

Nothing resembling resistance broke the quiet's spell. Even the twisting of a bottle cap and the filling of two glasses with a sliver of amber liquid couldn't make them abandon the shared hush. She placed a glass in Patrick's hand with care. His eyes went from the whisky to his friend's glass then back to his before finally settling on Marylynn's face. The consternation on her face resembled how Patrick felt.

He could think only of his able body, the strength and control it acquired and exhibited. Liquor had a reputation as poison. It caused ruin and broke down the body. Recalled tales of despair concerning the homeless people that littered the nearby big city of Valdosta came to mind. Any thought of his own physicality led back to Pastor Park. The sermon, the Bible verse that inspired the Pastor's philosophy, also the carnality once shared between teacher and student, all these things brought the face and figure of the Pastor like a fist to Patrick's gut. The relief from these blows colored the clear bottom of the glass in his hand.

"Bottoms up!" he commanded, then poured the swill down his throat.

The imbibed spirit proved stronger than one individual demon trapped inside Patrick. Though the oldest, it had no pretense of being the strongest. Three shots of whisky coursed like lava through his veins to warm his skin and melt his inhibitions. The bravery to divulge directly required half a bottle but Patrick stopped at the three measured pours. The careful crafting of his disclosure needed some lucidity. Marylynn kept on drinking. The drunkenness transformed her face into her mother's, minus the fury.

Telling his friend the truth about his adolescent desire towards members of his own gender terrified Patrick and affected him with a temporary stutter. Any twinkle of chance that Marylynn held onto with the hopes of lighting the way for a romance with Patrick died out, at last extinguished by an unmovable truth. Instead of trying to appear seductive or alluring, she switched modes to become a supportive friend. Threat with ulterior intentions for her politeness dissolved with every sentence he uttered. Marylynn understood Patrick could not be changed. This she found the most endearing even through pangs of defeat. At last, she understood her best friend.

Patrick left out any part about how he came to understand his inversion, or what he eventually began to call his grave sin. Once the talk turned to blaming the influence of invented devils, Marylynn told him he was crazy and that it's absolutely natural.

"Two of my uncles stay with men and nobody cares."

"But you know what the Bible says—" Patrick started before Marylynn cut him off.

"I don't give a damn about what the Bible says," Marylynn started. She gave pause for Patrick to respond and continued when he never did, "Look at what y'all's good book did to my mama…and look at what it's doing to you."

Patrick caught the double shock of her blasphemy, the truth behind what she said like a blow to the chest. The words he lined up to say only amounted to a less offensive comeback and not the one-two punch Marylynn delivered. He needed a new counter since the old one no longer stood a chance. Yet nothing sufficient came in time so Patrick relied on a defeated: "It's still wrong."

Three more shots of whisky apiece made them both forget the original point of their conversation. They hugged, collective tears running down their connected cheeks. The momentary memory loss increased the startling effect of any statement once the subject returned to their murky, drowned heads. Mention of Patrick's mama made him begin to imagine the shame his secret might bring to her already burdened life. He was now the ultimate encumbrance to her and himself, Patrick believed: a homosexual bastard. Comprehending that opened the floodgates for more tears. Marylynn thought she understood but she couldn't. Her mama's self-inflicted shame insisted everyone knew that disgrace except her mama.

The fear of ever being exposed, the repercussions, all added heat to the fire burning through Patrick's body. His stupefied mind gave poor instructions to his drunken body. Patrick stood up and left without saying a single word, just like Pastor Park during their earlier conversation that directly influenced the detrimental reveal just offered to Marylynn.

New eyes saw the same world for the first time. Processing responses to these augmented senses proved difficult for his new mind. Back roads never got much traffic, much to Patrick's good fortune. The sure, steady gait that moved him towards a new confrontation with Pastor Park existed only in his imagination; it was a miracle he remained upright, let alone on two feet. Some guardian angel kept his stumbling in check. Looking up into the sky, Patrick became astounded by the vision.

Rays from the setting sun peeked above the tops of dense pine trees. To his undone eyes, they became the arms of angels reaching down in extended grace to show a young man the error of his ways. While some of the arms bore lessons, others juggled eventual punishments that were sure to manifest if Patrick learned nothing from these examples. God's mysteries divulged themselves by His own design and demanded acceptance without question. This sober understanding carried over and affected Patrick's inebriation.

The light, though receded, kept its strong brilliance as it illuminated the world above Patrick's head. It would surely fade soon, but then another day began with the same light as a beacon to all. Some days stronger, or longer, or not much at all. But it was always a constant, all by the grace of God. If a gigantic star, millions of miles away, was a tool under His authority, then something lower, even a ruined boy like him, must realize his place and all that he owed to the Divine Will. Flawed in that present predicament, Patrick knew he carried little value to God, unable to serve while his body functioned for the basic desires of a poisoned mind. Pastor Park understood and taught only half of what Patrick needed to grow up able-bodied but then polluted everything. The man of God had become a venomous adversary. The last of the light overhead, the final act of supposed deific intervention imagined by a fevered and murky mind, stretched out one last glorious arm pointing the way to the parsonage.

Answering the door to an inebriated boy banging and yelling his arrival, Pastor Park stood by fixed in a listless stance while Patrick stammered and garbled with artificial audacity. The boy still had so much to say and did so with no regard to eloquence. The Pastor's perplexity only served to increase the boy's speaking volume. No part of it could be interpreted, success hinged on patience. Soon the man's tolerance began to ebb and dissatisfaction with the encounter passed between the two. The Pastor asked Patrick to leave.

Patrick refused after several suggestions. A conclusive clarity materialized. Not until Pastor Park told him the truth about his real relationship with "what's his name."

"I already told you I've never laid an inappropriate hand on that boy." Pastor Park stressed, barely able to entertain the inquiry with what little patience he had left.

"Just me, huh?" Patrick taunted, incredulously.

"Just you," the Pastor almost interrupted, "only ever you."

A swell of remorse rose in Pastor Park with the admission fresh from his mouth, never able to be unsaid. A reason why he made a lover of so young a boy never surfaced, and he had no time to contemplate or even fish for motives.

"What's to keep me from telling everybody you took advantage of me?" Patrick threatened.

Pastor Park's face flushed red, and he felt his steely resolve sink to his feet. Present fears mixed with similar panics dredged up from past indiscretions. Alchemy too advanced for a smalltown pastor to control.

"Patrick!"

Luann's voice cut through the atmosphere and sliced the tension in two.

Immediate shifts in demeanor jolted the Pastor and Patrick along with the shock of intrusion. A more presentable mask replaced what Pastor Park felt and wanted to express, suppressing it, and keeping it trapped inside. Patrick devolved into a literal sight manifested from the internal torment eating him alive. She ran to her crumpled son but looked to the stoic man of the house for answers.

"It smells like your son has had a little whisky." The Pastor kept any outward signs of disapproval in check, all the while wondering what Luann might have heard or seen. "Let me call someone to give you two a ride home. Please."

His insistence assured that his generosity was accepted.

Luann was grateful; she understood her frame held little support for her intoxicated, taller, and still growing son. More importantly, she betrayed no knowledge of her son's exchange with the Pastor.

Patrick lay on the couch during the wait. Heavy with drink and trouble, he succumbed to sleep. The adults spoke whispers in another room, away from the passed-out boy but within eyesight of both him and the driveway. The car summoned to take Luann and Patrick home had a short distance to cover, thankfully leaving no time for prolonged conversation. A mutual embarrassment lingered in the air along with the overpowering scent of whisky. No mention ever of Patrick's threat during the grown-up small talk. Pastor Park became certain it would be forgotten and slept off by the morning. A backup prayer later accompanied the hope as the Pastor prepared for bed. Just in case.

The next day brought presented troubles to the forefront that refused to be ignored. All situations insisted on involved secrecies as a necessary component for accomplishment. A fragile balance existed that kept order since neither of them held the capability to solve the equation alone. Luann knew nothing about her son's physical relationship with the Pastor while he never knew until too late that Patrick did indeed forget the threats, which meant he also forgot about telling his mama he was homosexual.

Luann feared the horrible thing she predicted about her son was true, it had been this way a while, but she didn't care to recognize it. Her son's affliction was inherited not only by the sins of his father, but those of his mother collided and combined to deal Patrick his own terrible lot. So much for a better future for her son, one like she once hoped for herself around his age, before she fell. She cried at the thought of her son now doomed for a life she imagined harder than her own. Any understanding of the perversion avoided comprehension even if Luann knew the cause. Sharing half the blame splintered a heart already broken in two.

The upcoming baptism would be a good beginning, Luann agreed with Patrick. Explaining to her son not to expect a miraculous and complete washing of his sin. Impiety would always be there, but water filled with the Lord's mercy offered a fresh start forgiven of sin, but never entirely. With God's direction, the boy was sure to correct the error of his ways then never harbor those impurities again with his mind and body focused solely on Him. More faith existed in that victory, Luann believed. Of the possible futures she pictured for her son, Patrick as a pastor never entered her mind.

A homosexual pastor. It helped so much make sense once Pastor Park resigned himself to the truth years ago. Submission never equaled acceptance. The discovered fact accounted for his reluctance to marry, and the church helped supplement deflection, serving as the perfect excuse. Pastor Park found women attractive but limited his experience with their pleasures to a single, fumbled incident. His devotion remained elsewhere until he met the perfect candidate and promising articulation of his philosophy of an able-bodied boy growing into a man. When God held total control of the Pastor's life, he became the perfect tool for divine dictates. His blemish proved too great at last, too powerful to stay dormant long. Policed and regulated in the past, the same could happen again. Turning his life back to God, being highly blessed and highly favored again, became the mission and what better way to start than bringing more of the flock to the pasture with the approaching baptism service he had planned.

How the Pastor failed to notice that very flaw in his protégé confounded him until he decided what held responsibility. Pride and his willful desire to create a masterpiece for God outside of himself. Why then did Pastor Park allow the relationship to become inappropriate, him being a man and Patrick still a boy? The Pastor faced a similar temptation once before and thankfully won the battle with the help of his own understanding Pastor. But that temptation existed before any trace of the impressionable, yet provocative youth named Patrick Owens marked the earth.

Only God can save me now, Patrick believed. Struggling with how he might single-handedly free himself from his sin, without involving sanctified hands, stole more than sleep. Conviction chipped away in bits as his waking hours grew to consume more of his nights. Deep in thought and holed up in his room, his mama observed and allowed her son's anguish until chores needed done around their own house.

"You don't have to go to the parsonage," Luann confirmed, still not privy to what caused the sudden cleft between her son and the Pastor, "but there's too much to do around here. I'm not working all day there then coming home to work when I should be resting. Especially with you around all day."

The movement did Patrick some good, but he still mostly kept silent, speaking only when spoken to, his replies clipped. All spare attention went towards his initiative to understand who he was, why he was, how to change it all, also, how to reacclimate into the same world as a whole new person. The process obligated that these inquests be solved in order. Patrick compared it to building a wall, each important brick needed precise placement before the next one could be laid, otherwise the wall's purpose and structure would be compromised.

After a week harrowing in a hell of his own design, Patrick slept like the dead. All questions had answers. A proper solution also hatched from so much incubated thinking in isolation. Understanding his sin, he knew how difficult life could be, how the likelihood of being ostracized threatened him if that life persisted. His betrayal by Pastor Park erased any trust bestowed upon that fallen man of God. The Pastor became a fetter, the start of a frayed loose end. Patrick and Luann needed to leave town. Youth granted the boy an exuberance for change, also a taste for impetuous urges. Impulsive, yes, but his mama also had a few years of youth left to squander. The change would do her good, too, Patrick resolved.

None of the particulars came to fruition without God's blessing. Every night on his knees, Patrick begged the Lord to make him whole and keep him from sin. In time, it seemed the efforts were rewarded. The Pastor fell further from the boy's considerations until the man and their past drowned beneath the flood of God's forgiveness. Petitioning the Lord with prayer went only part way and Patrick knew another step needed taking, one that brought him another step closer to heaven. He needed to be baptized, to be washed clean for a fresh start, body and soul. In the end, Patrick grieved, he needed Pastor Park to set him free.

Other than the seasonal event that had everybody getting dressed in the best of their Sunday best, the day differed little from any other. Vitality filled the hearts and quickened the step of those who planned to attended. Someone dared suggest it might be the Holy Spirit at work. The weather certainly bore the Lord's approval of the work about to take place in His name. The good Lord even kept the temperature hovering around eighty degrees and a cool breeze on hand for extra comfort.

After Sunday morning service, Pastor Park saw fit to test the waters at the pond. God provided a faultless pool for washing away the sins of His flock. Beyond a couple hour stay at the parsonage between then and his return, he remained close to the baptism site, tools and garb in readiness. Some time alone to recharge before the congregation again drained his energy. Their needs meant little beyond the baptism being another day of work. One among the probable attendees made demands of his hardships, unfair challenges. The variables involved kept the Pastor's attentions occupied. He thanked God baptisms were just another mundane aspect of the job, something even in his younger years he could perform in his sleep. The boy and his threats already stole too much of that and did not have permission to consume more of the haunted Pastor's life.

Options were weighed with care but with so much still vague on both sides, deciding became impossible. Personal feelings obfuscated the situation with their own complications. Betrayal never cut so deep before since love never bled out as a result. The Pastor knew his sins with Patrick wrought divine punishment and for that he expected fallout. Seeds of love grew in the Pastor's heart until the boy trampled what had been nurtured. Then the pain of Patrick's confession about what he witnessed reminded Pastor Park that not all the blame belonged to the boy alone. That ghost, or devil as Patrick described, showed no signs of ever going away. God would somehow see to it that waves of that anguish deranged him even in hell. The Pastor came to realize with finality that no future existed when parts of the past always haunt the present. The congregation began to arrive and mingle. The Pastor, once stopped by the first to show up, never knew another moment of solitude until right before the baptism began. Small talk made up the conversations, Pastor Park saw to that himself. He looked out for Patrick, or even Luann. When they showed up, Luann waited her turn to chat. Patrick never came close.

"Can we walk?" Luann asked when she was able. Pastor Park consented. Frantic nerves produced visible discomfort in a woman who knew how to conceal so much pain. Begging pardon for her nerves, she continued: "I have a question, Pastor Park."

Nervous disorder infected the Pastor, who stuttered as he spoke, thanks to thoughts of Patrick and his intimidation: "Yes. Anything."

"I know it's not my place to ask, even though as his mama I can't help but wonder about what happened between you and Patrick."

The first wave of reprieve fell upon the Pastor, too small for any significance.

"I just know that he hasn't been the same since." Luann's sincerity and understatement of her son's behavior threatened to bathe her in tears. She remained strong enough to go on: "He's a precocious boy, I know, but he's a good boy. I'm rambling, sorry. He wanted me to ask if it's okay for him to be baptized today, still…"

Color returned to the Pastor's face with a wash of relief. He quickly replied, though still through a diminished stutter.

"I can't refuse a request to bring somebody to God. Please tell him I will if he wants."

Luann appeared pleased by the response, even if inside she lamented the Pastor did not divulge the purpose of his fractured relationship with her son. She suspected with accuracy what she asked was not what Pastor Park expected to hear. His acceptance was nonetheless appreciated and shown with a nod.

At that, Pastor Park looked at his watch, then noted the time out loud before excusing himself to his preparations. This again elicited the exact polite nod from Luann as before and she walked one way towards her son while the Pastor went in another.

"Good afternoon, everybody. It's great to see you all again this afternoon. This is a special service in that my message will be strong but brief because y'all already got enough of my long-winded love for God only a few hours ago. God's will must be done instead." After a deep breath, he continued: "Nobody is perfect. Nobody here walks without sin. Even if you've been dipped in this very pond in the name of God Almighty and his son Jesus Christ, the stain of sin is still upon you. Upon us all. I'm not excluded. I'm a man of flesh and bone and nowhere upon my person is there a single, untarnished portion. But God saw fit to save this simple man and raise him up to be an example. I still fall short all the time, in my eyes as well as those of my friends. But I begin and end the day a man of God, who takes the flesh and bone and uses them for His divine dictates. Miracles exist. It's a miracle I've been able to serve him. I once was lost, found myself in a place I had no business being in, got out and got right with God. Though every now and again a devil from my past shows up to collect what's owed. No matter the toll on my flesh, my soul remains unbroken and in the hands of our Lord. Today I am here to deliver any and all souls to Him, in His name, and in the name of His son, Jesus Christ, and the Holy Spirit that surrounds us all, wherever and whoever we are."

The remainder of the concise sermon tied his usual message of being able-bodied seamlessly to the act of baptism and how it sealed the personal trinity of body, mind, and soul to themselves, then together again with the Holy Trinity of the Father, the Son and the Holy Ghost. Whispered amens escaped enraptured lips. A slight but sharp exhalation of air through Patrick's nose displayed his disbelief. Fortunately, nobody noticed, not even his mama. They still bought the lie Pastor Park sold. Patrick needed to keep belief that despite the Pastor's sins, God still imbued him with the power to forgive in His holy name. The flawed vessel still carried a few drops of holy water. God could use any instrument, no matter how blunt or unclean, for His work.

People started queuing up at the sermon's conclusion. Patrick deliberately lagged to get a place last in line. That position offered further time to mull over the myriad cogitations swirling around inside his head. He needed to figure out so much but soon gave up without ever trying. Emptying his mind of the buzzing activity proved beneficial. Attentions remained steadfast on the present task: baptism and the saving of his immortal soul. The scent of pine on the breeze blew away the last deliberations after he thanked God for its miracle, as he did with other natural interruptions. With God acknowledged as responsible for everything, his focus stayed fixed. In a way, by thinking of God, Patrick was thinking about his future. Nothing specific since he knew what the meek stood to inherit.

One at a time, the faithful met Pastor Park waist deep in the water to receive the Holy Spirit, to have their souls saved and fleetingly washed clean from the stains of sin. Each person presented a visible metamorphosis once they emerged from the momentary dip. It began to appear as though the Spirit leapt from the first to be baptized then on to the next, and so on, as excitement moved through the line back and forth, front to end over and over like a confined energy with no outlet. This communal power confirmed for Patrick that the Lord's presence was there that day to make good on the ceremony's promise. Soon, his name would be called to enter the water. The final blessing: he and Pastor Park's roads had no reason to ever cross again.

Patrick's name seemed to be called sooner than expected. Anticipation and tension stole time worse than laziness ever dared. His legs threatened to remain stationary but he swore he heard a heavenly voice instruct him along, it was time. Cool water sent a shiver through the boy. Increased proximity to the man who at once appeared as both temptation and savior made Patrick's blood run colder. Unease seized his muscles and again he froze, but only for a pause. The discernable voice of Pastor Park compelled him onward at last.

Closer to one another for the first time in weeks, a familiar intimacy still lingered as the space between them grew smaller. The Pastor's hand on the small of his back calmed Patrick and soothed away all his anxiety. A momentary lapse caused Patrick to remember and again crave a more devoted contact with the Pastor, how the arm that then supported his back once wrapped him tight in a bent version of affection. The temporary deceit to his soul felt good from phantom pains of profane love. In that instant, he knew he could never be free from his only real sin. The handsome embodiment of that wickedness would be the first person his eyes saw as he left the water, supposedly renewed. A burdened heart weighed heavy in the boy's chest. Rightly so if Patrick's new purpose and reason for being there was to focus on his soul. This threatened everything planned, intended or hoped as he began to see that future sink in that muddy water that supposedly possessed the power to cleanse. The obscurity at the bottom of the pool emerged with elusive allure.

"Patrick, do you accept Jesus Christ as your personal Lord and Savior?" Pastor Park's stutter returned.

"I do, Pastor Park."

"Patrick, I now baptize you in the name of the Father, the Son and the Holy Spirit, for the forgiveness of your sins, and the gift of the Holy Spirit."

With that, Pastor Park supported Patrick's full weight as the boy leaned back for submersion. The Pastor's other hand pressed firmly against Patrick's chest. A heartbeat felt steady and heavy through the thickness of damp clothing. The sun dealt a brilliant effect from its reflection against the rippled water. A moment to thank God granted the Pastor a rehabilitated vigor for the task at hand. The paradox of saving what he defiled weighed heavy in his soul, but God granted him the occasion to make it right, to set the impressionable youth back on the right path to glory. Both their futures showed no certainty of fulfillment, despite separate but mutual restored commitments to their heavenly father. Odds and probabilities changed color and shape like the light shimmering against his gaze from the undulating pond. What could Patrick do if he and Luann stayed in town? What could they do if they left? The misfortune of past mistakes already followed Luann like a tether, now added shame threatened to worsen an already ruined reputation. And what of himself? Could he stay and lead a church where he tarnished a boy who still had a couple years until he became a man? A swirl of options, opportunities, spinning like a roulette wheel. So much rode on outcomes and potential combinations. Gambles ended so fast that the consequences never had time to settle. Even more so with bad bets and losing rounds since the hand that held the Jack of Hearts lost more than the game.

The Pastor's right hand still covered Patrick's chest, but no life animated the muscle underneath. With all the force he could muster, he raised the boy out of the water. Standing him upright proved impossible with no consciousness to assist so Patrick slid back into the water, nearly submerging again before Pastor Park caught him to once more lift his head above the water. The dead weight of the boy caused the Pastor to fear the worst as he dragged Patrick to the shore of the pond.

Glassy, unresponsive eyes stared back in silent acceptance. Animation, passion, promise, all gone from a boy whose chance to benefit from these gifts never existed at all. Pastor Park prayed for a miracle despite knowing their futility better than most. Even with divine intervention the Pastor feared the consequences of his actions. Dead tongues articulated no indictments. Past sins surely forgiven still left a sticky residue the boy could never clear. The fate he dreaded began its slow resignation. Next steps mapped themselves without further provocation.

Luann's shrieking destroyed the afternoon's peace. Pastor Park attempted to resuscitate Patrick the instant he laid the boy flat at the water's edge. Grim reality settled over the flock gathered around the scene when all fell silent, even Luann who soon lost her voice from bawling. Questions kept stifled out of respect for the grieving woman and the man in whose arms her son had died. Then, an eruption. Fists replaced the voice in the assault Luann launched on Pastor Park. An appalling noise lurched from her throat instead of sobs. Most of the crowd waited with the hope that once Luann stopped pummeling the Pastor with closed-handed blows, her hands would open to rip the man to shreds. Pastor Park's resilience to those blows made Luann's ferocity more frenetic. Between the bawling and attacking, energy drained from the hysterical mother before the eyes of every astonished onlooker. She collapsed under the strain of physical and mental duress. A hush fell back over the gathered congregation as inquisitive gawking searched Luann for signs of life. More people pushed close and swarmed around the crumpled woman. The faint rising and falling of her chest convinced the people she still lived. Then all those faces searched among themselves for the already convicted guilty man, but he was nowhere to be found. Who would pay for the Pastor's sin? What happened next? What did Luann have to live for? These and other apprehensions dispersed into town along with the witnesses, speculated and spread like wildfire through dry pines.

Once home and in possession of enough wits, Luann became wracked with the unimaginable pain of losing a child. She stayed inconsolable and wide awake until an administered sedative helped her finally sleep. Marylynn kept watch through the night, even sleeping on the couch when the faint rattle of the screen door accepted the letter found later that next morning.

Luann read it over her breakfast. When the sender's identity became known to Marylynn, not even her surprise suppressed the need to know from being uttered aloud.

"How are you not upset?" Marylynn asked through her bewilderment. The marked difference in Luann's resolve scared her. "He can't invite you over to talk?"

"No. He left town."

That astonishing admission knocked any remaining words from her mouth, along with the wind reserved to float them out into the discourse. The will to wonder left. Marylynn recognized and respected Luann's silence and let the melancholy hang heavy over the rest of breakfast until it was time for her to go home. The quiet only dissipated during a discussion over dishes and when they said their goodbyes. Marylynn's promise to stop by later that afternoon got approved with a dubious smile from Luann.

Before the sun crowned the town at its glorious zenith, Luann knew the stinging smell that clung to her clothes would soon be detected from a distance. Each room of the parsonage wreaked of gasoline, an affront to the order she devoted her life to keeping within its confines. The heady scent nauseated her with unrepresentative sweetness to become one final thing these walls would never allow her to escape. Only when satisfaction with how she distributed the volatile liquid was met did she let herself remain still and in one place for more than a few seconds.

Once again, she read the letter Pastor Park left with cowardice wedged in the front door of her house. In it, the Pastor attempted to explain everything to the best of his ability. The fully divulged nature of his relationship with Patrick suggested heavier consequences. He allowed those sensations to lull him into what he came to realize was love, or something akin.

Only now do I realize that no matter what it was, it was wrong. Ungodly, in thought and deed.

It went on:

It's in my best interest to move on, to start over somewhere far away from Georgia where it'll be hard for my past to catch up. I know nothing will ever give you your son back, but I hope in time you'll be able to heal and also start life over somewhere else far away, where your past can't find you either.

That buoyant tone infected every word with an unintended insincerity. A man could shed his skin many times while constantly growing larger with lies and be brand new just like the snakes they so often acted like. A woman was always a woman, born to bear the pain of both raising men and suffering for having to do so. They weren't permitted to change, only adapt. Their skin grew tough and hard enough to repel soft touches. Her skin knew its stains, aware with the same sense of impermanence that clung to her clothes. Only one force of nature held the power to free her from herself, and to separate her from her past. Poignantly, it also lent a bold way to shape her future.

One last walk through the house, each room presenting memories to a mind muddled from toxic fumes. The kitchen where she cleaned before and after so many prepared meals. The living room where she sat and talked to Pastors past and present and where no more than three months ago her son repainted the walls. Their echoes bounced between rooms, down corridors and stairs. At first the more discordant reverberations blended without obvious atonality until their conflict entered the composition to make it unlikeable. The most pungent rooms held the worst retentions of her torment and the better part of all the gasoline that drenched the inside of the parsonage. The overpowering aroma flowed strongest from the master bedroom, where both she and her son lost their innocence to wayward men of God. That room she intended to annihilate.

All the self-inflicted blame, like all the trails of gasoline, led back to Luann, who stood calmly in the middle of the living room with her burdens ready to burn. She first failed herself when she accepted the lie from Patrick's father then let it flourish. The decision to stay and condone the abuse and serve her abuser had been made for her long before Patrick was born, before even she or her own mother were born. Botched efforts to make better choices extended their insidious reaching towards everything she did or attempted in the name of God. He failed her in accordance to how He failed all other women. Luann established that no other choice survived to improve her situation. In the end she still believed that she alone failed her son. Little pleasure came from the newfound knowledge of the ways in which God failed men. No more hanging on to inadequate endings. The time had come to gather the power for the greatest decision of her life. God destroyed Luann's world with water, so she set out to scar his with fire. A final satisfaction overwhelmed the woman, knowing she at least had some power to beat divinity to the first of many punches.

She watched as the tiny flame grew to consume the letter

Pastor Park offered as his excuse and condolences. Words meant nothing. She liked how the paper around them turned black to take them and their hollow meaning along to oblivion. Pain gripped her hand and never intended to let go. Luann wanted to feel it, to know an agony that might rival her failed femininity and the loss of her son. No matter what, she told herself, she wasn't going to scream. There were no tears left to shed. *Good thing,* Luann reasoned, *I don't want anyone to see me cry ever again.*

Soft winds fanned the flames once they consumed the parsonage. A pillar of smoke from the inferno scattered ashes over a modest radius from the source. With that fire, Luann increased her notoriety instead of the erasure she desired. Fire transfigured her and Patrick's story, especially the last spring, summer and early fall of their parallel lives. Every inexorable rumor that never went away during their lifetime was now free to inspire the stuff of rural legend.

1 JOHN 3:15

"Everyone who hates his brother is a murderer..." 1 John 3:15

HE JUST stood there, watching. It's the one thing I remember most from the entire incident. The fists to the face, kicks to the groin or gut, and the rain of spit have lost any lasting sting or stain. Wounds of degradation eventually heal, then fade. Green eyes glared back anytime my own found his stare. Since he did nothing to help, it meant my brother approved. That bruise never disappeared like the others. Long after the fact, phantom pains still hurt enough for me to prefer an actual heart attack.

If anybody's gonna kick your ass, it's gonna be me! The mantra got old the second time I heard it. That day proved it a lie. I never associated truth with my older brother, but it was understood he would protect me since he has always been twice my size. I can count on half a hand the number of times he came to my rescue after that but too little, too late. The damage had already been done, exacerbated by injuries sustained anytime he kept the threatening part of his promise.

My grudge never kept me from being civil anytime we saw each other, but after we were all grown up it did keep those reunions brief. Thankfully, his tolerable daughter didn't inherit too much of my brother's ignorance. I'll never understand why she loves him so much. An absent man glares back from all her memories, just like our own father does. Hope continues living in her heart, kept apart from any outward denial. How many hours has she wasted wishing he would be the parent she wants and feels she deserves? She first revealed these secrets to me when she was fifteen, an hour after she got home from having an abortion, a baby pregnant with a baby. I had to swear I'd never tell her dad and I never have. Nor have I ever felt the need to commiserate and tell her how he let me down, too. His narrow-mindedness has always hurt the ones he should love.

We all "loved" my brother at a distance. Mom gave up on him sometime during his twenties, dad did too but earlier. I never liked him now that I look back. We fought even more than brothers tend to do. One and a half years separate us, but a more oceanic gulf always made seeing eye to eye impossible. The one time I wanted his help the most, he was miles away, even though he was standing mere feet from the scuffle.

Self-centered and never generous, excess was welcome, but only if it benefitted him alone. That more was never enough for him was unmistakable, considering his poor choices. He was addicted to the worst of things, and his additions took full advantage of him. He didn't pursue anything if it involved too much work. It's easier to steal, drink, and do drugs than be responsible – a tired ideology with a subscription he renewed for many years, ever since the age of fifteen.

Understanding why he never liked me has always been easy. He's a real man and doesn't think I am or ever can be, considering whatever criteria constitute his standards. But I can never understand why, or how, he just stood there and watched me being beaten. No emotion showed on his face or behind his eyes. Flashes of cold green streaked between darker green grass and a clear, cerulean sky. Each glimpse made me shudder against the late spring heat of South Georgia. The thick smell of copper filled my nose and ran into my throat. It felt as if it was in my lungs, everywhere, that strange, clean odor and taste of blood. What did I really do to deserve his indifference? What did I really do to deserve the beating my brother witnessed? I didn't stare at any of them in the locker room. I didn't want to do to them what they suggested. They were stupid and ugly just like my brother. I told them so. Insulting their mothers didn't help.

So many people watched me get beat up and did nothing but enjoy the spectacle. None of those people mattered back then; I couldn't recall any of their names or faces if I tried. I wanted to forget my brother after that day, but living under the same roof made the endeavor impossible. After a while I quit wondering why, the reward not worth the effort. It is sometimes easier to forget when comprehension or forgiveness are impossible. A persistent theory of mine is that he wanted to witness someone else do what he wasn't allowed to do to me. Our mom would've killed him if he even hit me once and half as hard.

His green eyes have dimmed over the months, but there's a flash of something I recognize from our younger days, back when his appreciation for life was still active. His desire to live has been restored, but too late. Life is slipping away from him every day. Without a stem cell transplant, his chances to live diminish exponentially. His daughter can't donate, she isn't a match. She was the first to offer. Out of duty to our mom I had my blood tested only to have my biggest fear confirmed. An exact match. But I refuse to donate, past anemic blood issues from birth and how I can't even donate blood are more than acceptable excuses. For anybody else in the family, I'd deeply consider it and depending on who it was, even go through with the procedure. I'm confident enough in my health as an adult to know I'd come through it all safe and intact. For my brother however, my mind was made up the instant the doctor announced the need. I saw his eyes searching wildly among the small gathering of family, hoping to catch my gaze with a beseeching glare.

All this makes me watch him now with the same indifference with which he watched me. My real feelings are never exposed. My icy blue eyes have been trained to never betray their unkindness. The lack of concern I feel while looking at him hooked up to so many wires and tubes liberates me. The only time I was alone with him here in the hospital, I laughed at the thought of the giant beeping machine being the only thing in the room wanting him to live.

I visit infrequently, not because of guilt but because I get no pleasure in bearing witness to his slow decline. Being scarce also keeps me from having to deal with my niece, whose own green eyes would sometimes fix on me with the same contempt killing my brother. Now her father is at death's door. My refusal, not wanting to even try and save his life has set a coldness growing inside her and now she extends it to me. I can tell my niece secretly pines for a day to come when I might need her to save my life. That day will never come. She'd be the last person I'd ever ask, even I could bring myself to think of her as a last resort. Besides, I'll outlive her and her resentment.

Fairness plays no part in my decision to deny my brother another chance at life. He doesn't deserve it and I don't deserve to suffer for his benefit. As a grown man, I don't answer to anybody, nor am I responsible for anyone's life but my own. No kids look to me for nurture, so the sight of my brother's silent pleading comes off as vulgar and bratty.

His final display made me most comfortable with my choice. In refusing him while he's dying, I'm doing what I never could when he was at full strength. I was never able to beat him at anything, especially a fight. He was always twice my size. Now his body is withered by disease. If we ever fought back then, I'm sure I would have tried to kill him because of all the animosity reserved just for him. Now I can do it. No contact, just a decision made while concealing a smile.

The more I think about it, the better I feel about my decision to not visit anymore. The shame is long gone and soon my brother will be too. I won't care when he goes, just like he didn't care that I left on what will become the last time I saw him alive.

CEMENT HORIZON

GRAY BUILDINGS reach in vain towards glory blocked out by grayer skies. Damp and chill blight this day in June. But here I am for a month. The train arrives just before noon and I'm on the street quicker than I expected to be. The street foods combine to create such a wild aroma that I'm instantly hungry. But, first, I need to check in to my hotel. I appreciate that it's only two blocks away.

The lobby appears unchanged from when a famous scientist lived there, which made me think of my own work. Each floor ascended lifts ideas into the swirl already active in my head. The nineteenth floor, room 1939 to be exact. I'm in New York, at the New Yorker Hotel, to write a novel. I look out my window and see the top quarter of the Empire State Building down 34th Street, and now I'm certain of success.

A block west on 34th Street to 9th Avenue waits the best fix for the famished: Golden City Chinese Restaurant. Quick, easy, nourishing, and delicious takeout. Even the name Golden City belies the gloom cast over New York. I opt for the old favorite of ginger chicken and an order of chicken fried rice. Within ten to fifteen minutes, I'm out the door due east, back to the hotel.

The food lasts less than ten minutes. Travel always makes me hungry. The surprise of two fortune cookies makes me wonder if they thought the meal was for two. I'll still eat both. *You'll soon get good news over the phone.* That sounds promising even if I don't believe these things. Seems generic. *Tomorrow's*

144

your lucky day. More generic. Again, my reason here, to write a book, remains my top priority, should a call I have scheduled work out well. No time for a new friend but plenty of time for good news over the phone. I'm torn whether to invest the energy to believe or not, because to have faith in one means they all deserve the same respect. I go about the afternoon and evening giving the subject or prospect little consideration.

Early to bed, early to rise, and all that. Barely out of the shower, my phone rings. A call from a potential publisher. A meeting with the company is already in the schedule but an excited urgency explains the anticipation to meet on both sides. In ten minutes, I go from prospective, past probable and into the realm of certain publication. They like my pitch more than I expected.

"Is today too soon?" they ask.

"No, of course not. Just tell me when and where."

The restaurant lies five blocks north and a couple east in Bryant Park. The representative I meet, one Stephen Charles Reid, talks excitedly about how great he expects my book will be, why they want to publish it, and how do I get my ideas, anyway? Everything in this city moves fast, from cars to hours to mouths, and I find it hard to keep up. "I'll do my best," I promise. He must sense my disorientation because he starts asking questions so that I feel more involved.

"I plan to write, not much else," I insist.

"Good," he returns. "Let's meet again in a week. Same time and same place."

Later that evening, after walking around the neighborhood to see where I'm living for the next month, I get hungry again. Back to Golden City to order the same thing I ate yesterday.

And again, I find two fortune cookies in a bag filled with enough food for two. *Find a new reason to smile every day.* I change that to find a new reason to write every day. Smiling doesn't come natural to me. Not really a fortune but a message. *Something you want is just within your reach.* More inspiration to consider rather than a fortune but it makes me remember the two from yesterday. In a way, they both came true.

During the week, I write all I can. Fast-paced walks help when the sentences slow. My explorations begin to lead from the area around my hotel, beyond its confines. I walk along the paths of fellow writers who lived on West 43rd Street between 8th and 9th Avenues or had sex with strangers just outside Chelsea at 28 West 28th Street, and further afield to hunker down in a bunker and declare war on words. What do I expect to happen, following in the footsteps of fallen angels? Who am I to think I can figure out what they couldn't? What do I have to prove? Do I want to stand taller than the skyscrapers? Aim for the moon, die among the stars, or whatever. No wonder so many who try end up a shit stain on the bed they die in, or a smear of blood on the pavement. Hard not to fall trying to rise above so much steel and concrete. And with overcast skies, up looks like down and no other direction makes sense. Falling down, falling forward or just falling behind?

Those quandaries aside, I make impressive progress with the work. Re-reading portions, I recognize that a few of those queries leaked into the lines and leeched their sour dispositions onto the characters. I like this development. So does one Stephen Charles Reid. After I slide what I've finished so far across the table, his astonishment surprises me. A quick glance becomes complete immersion for three entire pages. His warm praise leaves a twinkle in his eyes as we order. I look up at the waiter to order and words won't come out, in spite of my mouth going through the appropriate motions.

The boy's beautiful face smiles with angelic patience, stealing more time from my words. Eventually, I manage to order, and Stephen follows, oblivious to my sudden captivation. The waiter writes our orders down with quick, skillful hands, and his soft lips say it back with precision. In the minutes he stands by our table, I try and take in what I can, to remember for dreams. His square jaw moves nicely when he speaks or smiles. A military haircut, like a blond crown, spikes and circles his head. So much about the boy—Joseph, according to his name tag—appears square, solid, and stable. Muscles knot in his arms when he writes, or in his shoulders when he laughs at my lame jokes. God, I want him to always be smiling. I watch as he walks away, admiring what I couldn't see while he stood facing us. The entirety of his perfect, cornfed body suggests sports throughout high school and college while also reassuring me that those years aren't too far behind him.

Transferring the conversation back to my pages with Stephen is easy; fixing on them long enough to forget a single thing about Joseph – not so much. The distraction gets explained away as inspiration, the truth after all. The way he looks at me, I swear he looks into me. Can he see my lust, my complete and utter awe? Sure, he does, he even flirts back. His smile becomes smug whenever we exchange words. With his cute, upturned nose scrunching up a bit more and a deliberate revision of his grin where only one corner of his mouth lifts, I fall into something deeper than lust but far shallower than love.

I carry thoughts of Joseph back to my room, constituting

memories grounded in reality and stirred fantasies. I figure writing is the only way to get my mind off of him, so I sit at the desk to begin. Two forgotten fortunes from last night's takeout mark my place in the notebook. I have no memory of what they say, nor any real recollection of getting food since the only words or actions important before pertained to my writing. *A new friend is about to enter your life.* I want to believe. Truly. And thinking about Joseph in this moment, I want to even more so. But I refuse to misplace hope since there's so little to go around. *Tomorrow's your lucky day.* Something is fucking with me. I can think of no other explanation. I recognize the second fortune as a repeat. Since I don't believe in fate or chance or even god, the universe holds no blame. Solid science and facts only. I believe in atoms and black holes.

So, when my legs bring me back to the restaurant at Bryant Park where Joseph is still working, I'm not sure what will happen, but I decide it worthy of a conclusion. From my vantage point at the bar, I see Joseph shuffle past for a couple of hours of his shift. Any time our eyes lock, he flashes that exuberant smile and a part of him dissolves into me, swear to god.

Two nursed beers later, I go and sit on the periphery of the restaurant, waiting for anything involving Joseph to happen. Soon I'm no longer satisfied with just thinking about him. I want to talk to him, one-on-one, and get to know him. All our flirtatious grinning makes me close to a hundred percent sure he thinks the same way, or maybe even wants the same thing. After an hour of deliberation splitting my head in halves of longing and doubt, I go back inside to get his number, or at least see him again. But according to the bartender Joseph has left for the day.

Anything I put on paper reads like garbage, sounds forced and uninspired. All I want is Joseph. Beside me, under me with me inside him. The pen's might pales compared to the terrible swift sword between my legs. Night falls and the lights below block out any stars bright enough to pierce the clouded skies. Out my window and down 34th Street the tip of the Empire State Building glows, more alive tonight than me.

When I turn the lights off, the scene outside the window gains an even more astonishing radiance. Colors shift and splash on the room's walls and even my skin appears to transfer between different hues. Clusters of dusky buildings loom in the darkness of gloaming despite jutting from the rippling light below like a craggy coastline. The spire of the Empire State Building illumines safety and surprise to travelers and citizens alike. Sitting down on my bed, my view limits knowledge of the swirling neon underneath. Rooftops and sky remain discernable.

Out there in the 23 square mile expanse of somber concrete and schist Joseph eats, drinks, lives, and sleeps. Too much ground to cover on foot but from up above the chances of seeing him or being seen increase. Encountering Joseph again tomorrow becomes my priority until the sights I stole of him and stored in my brain remind me of their baser purposes. Within seconds my underwear falls around my ankles and I lay back on the bed. Spit glistens to better reflect the lights screaming from the streets down below. My own great erection lines up perfectly with the iconic skyscraper visible just outside, now framed between my legs and window. Frustration, apprehension and so many other fears come streaming out, warm and opaque. An invigorated sense of resolution sends me to sleep and blesses my rest with fitful but elaborate dreams.

Instead of eating at the restaurant where Joseph works, I opt for a quick meal at Golden City. A few steps away from the door the clouds open up to let the sun wave at anyone lucky enough to notice. But with matching abruptness, the clouds again rob another summer day of its promise.

I pay little attention to the meal itself. My two new fortunes inform me of expectations and their plausible outcome, therefor they stay with me longer than the calories. *Something you want is just within your reach.* I like the idea of so much promise on that tiny strip of paper. *Find a new reason to smile every day.* Another repeat but since I altered the one before, this comes across as a new admonition. Too good to be true, like I've come to expect.

The next few days, I linger at the tables across from the restaurant where he works, but I don't see Joseph. I'm too distracted and my writing shows. My notebooks accompany me on these vigils and I'm confident that motivation will move me when I see Joseph, but I never do. Hope can go to hell.

I just want to see him again, to be seen by him again, to feel like I have even a little relevance to him. But I don't know him, or whether or not he works here anymore. The possibility only exists briefly and how easy to feel the opportunity already passed. But it could still happen. And maybe this time when hope follows me out of hell, I won't turn around like a dumbass.

Thank god I'm a dumbass. I know he could have slipped past my noticing because after sitting for over an hour, the desire started to go. His beauty is increased tenfold thanks to my yearning for all of him: every aspect of his being, every facet of his mind. The empty bar offers an easy seat and from there I see Joseph when he passes. New details join my memories, revitalized by the boy's constant back and forth.

The next day I find myself back again, but don't see Joseph. Stephen looks across the table with dismay at the scant few pages I provide. It's not just bad, he says, it's also so little, he insists. Then he asks about the passion that moved and informed the previous prose. The constant shifting of my gaze, unable to settle on any one thing for very long in case Joseph shows up, explains more about my distraction than my mouth dares to confess. By the end of our lunch meeting, I still haven't seen who I want. To shift his disappointment into hope, Stephen glides the conversation towards something less critical and asks me out for dinner. I smile, thank him politely, yet decline, but not before my body language gives my answer away before it's expressed. A quick lie about needing the time to write fails to work on him. He insists that I need to eat. All that makes me think about is how I want to consult the oracle making fortune cookies for Golden City. A raincheck for some other night satisfies Stephen. A follow-up lunch to discuss progress in two days' time mollifies us both. I really want to impress him and make a promise to do better that I'll half-keep. I head to the hotel after lunch.

I do get hungry later, though my empty notebook open on the desk is more deficient than my stomach. Off to Golden City and back to fill my belly and the depleting coffers of potential. *A new friend is about to enter your life.* Dammit! Another repeat. So much for encouragement. A machine must churn these out at random from a selection of phrases, reproduced ad nauseum. No portending beyond however many preprogrammed destinies. But a gnawing desire reminds me that it is by chance that these messages entered my life in the first place. So, for now I'll take them for more than they're worth. I could use good luck.

And certainly, the second time getting this message heralds Joseph's readiness to meet me. *You are heading towards a choice between money and happiness.* A new one, and not generic like the others. Choices indicate abundance. I can't be picky; I'll take whatever comes my way. Will I be happier with Joseph or better off with money from the book? I never thought I'd have to decide, so I vow to achieve both. In two days, I'll see Stephen again, impressing him with what I will produce between now and then. Then I'll finally meet Joseph because if I want him bad enough, we will happen. I wanted a book deal more than anything and here I am – but that was before I wanted Joseph.

Words drip more than flow while the leaden firmaments of day give way only to a deliberative night. I walk to keep my mind on writing when the prose won't come. Again, up and down streets, through avenues where so many before me lived, loved, and lost their lives. How easy to think you can be a part of it all when faced with the largesse of this city, that greatness transfers symbiotically. Quick comes the truth that nobody is necessary. The city goes on without you. Sometimes it rolls over you, compacting person to pavement. Still the people look up and want to be a luminous star against the night sky. Real stars are impossible to see in New York at night. The dull day atmosphere holds no blame. Only the vortex of the city really knows why. Surrounding radiance gets sucked into the center, geographically in the southern part of Central Park. Here, everything moves at such a great speed that time feels the effects. This city, this slate gray black hole, drives so many people mad. Once over the edge, there's no going back.

Good feelings follow me to my next lunch with Stephen. He notices a difference in my demeanor, and also my prose.

An improvement all around, he assures. Smiles bounce back and forth between us, infusing us both with unearned audacity. Stephen wonders out loud about what I have planned later. Writing is all, I confirm. Maybe a walk. The question is raised: whether I want company or not? A joke would fall flat right now considering the look of intent covering his face. Why not, I say to a smile that then immediately doubles in size. The thought of a brief respite from thinking too much about Joseph appeals to me. My mind yearns to think of something else, someone else. Stephen seems interesting when I look past all the business energy he exudes. I want to know his story, to see if any part of it mirrors my own.

But as we get up to leave, our heads turn in unison towards the shouting of an argument. And without any manifest intent on my part, all I can now think about is Joseph. With a furious flash, he flings his apron at the recipient of his insults. The poor man never manages a word between Joseph's yelling and his sudden departure. Looks like my walk with Stephen starts now.

West on 40th. Between the wind rushing between the clamor of traffic and my severe focus on keeping up with Joseph, I hear only bits of what Stephen says. My attention swings from the beautiful boy ten feet or so from us to Stephen, in the middle of a barely interesting anecdote about the New York Public Library at Bryant Park. I love history but the need to know more about Joseph overrides the desire for much else. Through wretched Times Square full of glassy eyed tourist and glossy imbeciles then south on 8th Avenue. I mention my hotel to Stephen as we walk past and he smiles, then nods, taking note.

Entering Chelsea makes me hopeful, still in pursuit of Joseph. This means that some possibility exists, he just needs to see me. Or better, know me. Once my head becomes too full of his splendor and of baited promises, I look at Stephen. Still handsome in his early fifties, living and working in the city has been kind to him. Not dating much is the secret, he confides, and laughs. Catching my breath when we finally stop at a crosswalk, I understand this as I watch Joseph disappear into the 23rd Street subway station.

A good place to turn around, I suggest. Stephen handles the conversation and I listen, this time with more intent. The gaps in what I recall from anything he said earlier doesn't go unnoticed. My apology works to calm him down. I also make a promise to always pay better attention. Compromise never sits well with me, so I'm curious to see how well I'll keep my word. And the consequences of a promise become subjective between two people who can't even agree on the definition of a great novel. Joseph is far from my mind a block after we turn around to head back north.

And only once do I think of Joseph when we enter the hotel restaurant and walk past the bar. The arrangement of bottles and glasses resemble the setup of the restaurant he quit earlier. I settle for a beer that I nurse for the hour and a half it takes Stephen to guzzle three rum and cokes. Liquid encouragement but for what? I ask him. His smile is confused smile, and he is unable to make up his mind, fluttering between what to believe, and what to make of a double-edged question of dubious meaning. Nerves that never calmed from the alcohol ruin any bravery coursing through his veins, en route to merely damage his liver. Profuse apologies follow Stephen's vows of more professional interactions going forward. Once I convince him of no harm, no foul, he can't seem to get out of the restaurant fast enough. The need for greasier food than this menu allows becomes the reason I suggest Golden City a block away.

I'm trapped on the nineteenth floor to work, but all my mind wants to worry about lies sprawled two hundred feet below. Somewhere out there, Joseph resurfaced from the subway and left my life forever. Reasonable doubt suggests our paths have no basis to ever cross within any square mile of this island. An insidious force struggles with all its might to not be seen. What once held so much wonder – lights, noise, people – becomes obnoxious and common this far inside the perpetual shadow of the city. Cement crowds the horizon, well beyond what the eye can see from ground level or even perched above in a hotel room. Foreboding gray skies add mystery to where anything begins or ends. We lose ourselves and *become* no longer detectable or knowable once inside, not to anyone or anything, including ourselves. Bodies and souls bend and transition, folding in halves until finally vanishing. Any assurance made to stay unchanged, to come out the same way I went in, collapses under so much gravity.

All because of a cliché – the attention of a guy. If I can impress him or whoever his replacement might be, then I can impress upon the city at large some semblance of success. I think I have it backwards, actually. Sadly, I confess that I'm losing direction, the compass not working right since I stepped off the train. No rest, minimal sleep, too many demands, all so the same actions can get repeated to grind the spirit before the body, to make a disappearance easier.

Somehow the maelstrom of feelings finally knocked the power out in my brain, helping me sleep through the night until just before noon. A grateful body responds with hunger lacking anxiety. Off to Golden City for food and fortune. *Someone close to you is jealous.* Stephen? Joseph? I don't really know either, but I guess I know Stephen more. But he doesn't know about Joseph. Well, we did follow Joseph yesterday for fifteen blocks and more than once Stephen made a comment about my loose attention. I understand now. *That person you thought your enemy will do something nice.* No enemies in New York City cross my mind, but if pressed, maybe this could refer to Stephen upset by my rejection. He has been nothing but nice already. I refuse to think about the interpretations and regret they're not the generic fortunes requiring little contemplation.

Instead, I'd rather think about coincidence, or happenstance. So, I do for the rest of the day and on into the next; I think because of Joseph, it must be because of him. But I don't figure out why, knowing him now only as a magnificent memory. Who cares, I'm hungry. Golden City will be an option today with fuller clouds crowding the atmosphere. Stepping outside the hotel, I stare up at the relentless gray heavens and imagine the sun only shining on Joseph since the sun must only show his face to the deserving in this city. I only remember seeing it a couple times.

Stephen walks up and says hello before I turn right to start down 8th Avenue. All I want to think about now is coincidence until he mentions the amount of time he spent standing outside, knowing I'd probably come out soon for food, possibly. He proceeds to apologize for his behavior from yesterday. Anything I try to say gets blocked by a question from Stephen. Are you hungry? How's the writing? How'd you sleep? Nerves hiccup the flow of his inquiries. My answering calms him to a degree. I am hungry. The writing's coming along. I slept okay.

The restaurant sits us immediately. No Joseph here, obviously, but feel his ghost whenever any of the cute waiters saunter past. They all pale in comparison but could be him to someone else dining here today. Realizing this from the start makes it easier to focus on Stephen. He stumbles his way through the plans for my book once it's ready then sweetens the deal with talks of the publishing company wanting another because certainly the first one will sell well. I like how this all sounds. The desire for readers outweighs the desire for money, but why not both?

When talk turns to the writing, I excitedly tell Stephen about the nature of happenstance and how thinking about it and living it influenced the narrative of the novel. In turn, he becomes more excited. Politely waiting until I finish, Stephen speaks a little about his thoughts on coincidence and how something profound happened yesterday after we parted ways. I'm intrigued, to say the least.

After crying into his Chinese food, because all he could think about was how he might've upset or offended me, the waiter brings him his check and a fortune cookie. He insists on not giving much thought to the messages inside, but he found it impossible to ignore this one. *A new friend is about to enter your life.* Needing more guidance and clarity, Stephen asked for another cookie. *Tomorrow's your lucky day!* All signs point to me, Stephen insists. I fight back the urge to laugh.

These exact two fortunes I also received on the same visit once before. No way I'll tell Stephen, but the correlation catches me. I wonder if my messages were meant to be about Stephen instead of Joseph. I heaped my own desire and promise on an unobtainable object. Stephen knows I'm obtainable to a degree. His choosing to concentrate that deliberation on me makes sense. That doesn't mean it's fair. I listen to him inject philosophy with extra aspiration in order to solve a more material problem.

I have a lot to think about as he walks me back to my hotel after we eat. My own opinions are overcast and pressure compounds me further into more quandaries. Somewhere in the middle of my soul rests real understanding of how to respond. It's too dark in there and I'm afraid either way. So, I rely on immediate assessment to take control. I understand desire. I understand ulterior motives. And I understand using a situation as a means to an end. Such comfort comes from knowing eventually everything ends. I invite Stephen upstairs to take a look at the progress I've made with the novel. The threat of rain a solemn promise.

After Stephen leaves my room, I start writing. I do not see the sun set directly, only the broad glow lifted from the street. My concentration jumps out of the closed window, so I follow to look out and see where it might've landed before losing its mind among the people and noise. I feel in the middle of a chaotic universe, but I also feel nothing. A big city of overcrowded sensations tries to force itself inside my room. My favorite artist said success is a job in this city and soon my book will be available in stores all across the island and beyond. Success. Most people, if they hoped for any of this, would surely expect to see hope in hell.

Natural light retreats, replaced by artificial delights and illusion. Already an altered sense of self hovers on the other side of my window and stares banefully back. Recognition never comes thanks to artifice throwing distortions against the glass. I grow to like it and how the face looking back never fully resembles my own. Coincidence stops mattering. Joseph loses importance. Stephen already started fading the moment I came. Who the hell am I? A soon to be published writer.

My struggles, past, present, and future, now belong to this city. A debt I can never repay grows every second until I pass beyond the event horizon and dissolve along with the rest of the light and debris. The writers who walked these streets before, searching for their own unique victories, did god-knows-what for lord-knows-who to move even an inch closer to winning. Their impressions still stamp the sidewalks and name the skyline. Trapped in all that metal, steel, glass, and stone, but out in the open for all to see and know is ambition. One more name will be in lights, then another, then this star rises while that other implodes. This must all seem stellar from the outside looking in. Who knows how any of this appears or even what, if anything, can be seen, considering the lengths we will all go sometimes to not be visible.

THE SINS OF OUR FATHERS, WHO AREN'T IN HEAVEN

DAN SAT in silence, listening but not hearing, looking but not seeing, smiling but not caring. The holidays had not mattered since his childhood when an ideal family existed on the surface. Christmastime indicated the fake, indifferent situations staged by his family until his parents split. A marriage that had no business happening at all lasted long after the spirit of the institution faded. Separate but together and never in love. Unlike Étienne's parents. Dan felt the devotion Françoise still had for her departed husband. It was a love he recognized in flashes when Étienne looked at him. But that family disintegrated long ago and the only person who ever made them memorable died a couple months before he found himself half-interested with his in-laws. Food abounded, spread out across the length of the table, even options for Dan's picky palate. The accommodations were appreciated. A full belly meant the nod of an imminent nap helped detach him. The practice of presenting an ideal family kept him from catching too much notice among the gathering of twelve.

Not contributing to the conversation meant little expectation and even fewer attentions. The sparse Christmas lights strewn about the house as customary decorations Dan found offensive. Not as in poor taste, but because they represented an artificiality that stood for something larger than its meager glow conceded. The brightest light in his life had been extinguished only recently so anything outside of him where that radiance once blazed with intensity paled, if it ever even registered. His words stayed few and polite yet reeked of liquor. Time drowned in a brown still of cognac, preserved instead of lubricated, and the hour approached with little urgency when Dan and his husband Étienne left for home.

Being neither heard and not really seen given his aloofness, Dan's attentions shifted with ease from one conversation to the next. Everything within earshot bored him all the more, from worries about finishing Christmas shopping in time for the big day to pot shots at Françoise's cooking travelled in one ear and out the other. Dan became too uninterested to even nap. Cognac and wine loosened lips and lowered reservations but so much of the banter proved annoying. Just then he heard Françoise's voice slightly above the clamor from the other guests. Her fussing over something held Dan's interest for a moment before it began again to move on to another dull dialogue. Françoise laughed nervously. The uniqueness of tone brought Dan's attentions back just in time to hear her say, "*Merde!* Only made that mistake once and boy did your father let me have it. And HARD!" Dan turned around to see Françoise standing close to her son. He had no idea what she almost did wrong, but the look on both men's faces exposed their acknowledgment of what she said. Flushed, she offered a rash explanation: "It happened one time. Your father hit me one time. It was no big deal. Actually, kind of funny like in a French gangster movie. *Rififi* or something." Françoise believed through her cognac that the explanation satisfied the two men, fortunately the only two who seemed to have heard. A nervous exchange of discomforted glances passed between the three, nobody knowing what to say or do next. Then, as if nothing unusual had happened, Françoise went about her business. Dan wanted to ask what she was talking about but knew to let his husband inquire about his own family. And Étienne never questioned, but only continued to imagine.

Shortly thereafter, his husband noted Dan's capacity for a public nearing full and offered a gracious excuse to start the process of leaving. So many hugs and several "*Oh, encore une chose*" too many tried the muscles keeping Dan's face frozen in a stupid smile. Soon everyone would know how being annoyed and ready to leave might make him start the journey to the car in the middle of his mother-in-law's prattle. It sounded beautiful and Françoise looked gorgeous in her designer dress, but the time had come and gone. On cue, Françoise said a goodbye she actually meant. Her son always got the first hug, the leftovers-of-a-weak-hug reserved for the spouses of her children like Dan. But this auxiliary hug lingered, the embrace more firm and sincere. From his chest Dan heard sweet condolences rise upward to his ears.

"Thank you, ma'am." Dan proclaimed, his southern accent and manners on full display. Extra care was also taken to avoid indicating any lingering embarrassment from the earlier situation.

"You don't have to call me ma'am," Françoise responded. "You can call me Françoise. Alors, you can even call me Maman."

The innocent sincerity touched Dan and his response surprised even him. "Those are some awfully big shoes to fill."

There could never be a replacement. Once the sun exploded, the moon had nothing to reflect, therefor no illumination to offer at all. Françoise, a minor actress in a couple of French New Wave films from the early sixties, knew her cues well.

"I'm not trying to be a replacement. Not even a substitute or stunt double. But I can be a surrogate if you'd like." Her command of the English language always betrayed by a thick accent and often not knowing the right word to use as a descriptor. "Just try me," she concluded with one final hug that summed up the love a mother could have for a child. Dan left the house unsure if the gesture came from a genuine place of compassion or was just a means to make nice in light of her accidental confession. Determination to find out compelled him to appreciate the offer.

Once out of earshot, Étienne announced: "And you'd better tell me if she ever brings *that* up again."

The weekly calls began with the formality of a promise kept in earnest. Dan's gratitude grew immediately and after only a couple of calls, familiarity developed. Calls on Sundays began to last longer than a polite half hour. The inner workings of Françoise, or of himself, just weren't that interesting. And the calls soon went from being for his benefit to becoming a channel for Françoise's grievances. Dan found it amusing when the realization dawned.

Conversations graduated to include an occasional barb at a family member Dan never knew. Once an initial complaint about her daughter and the fact a grandchild had yet to be produced became exacerbated by an unintentional question from Dan. That caused the dam to burst. Every conversation thereafter contained more and more muck from the stagnant water dormant for an inordinate amount of time. Finally, Françoise had an outlet. When that swamp eventually drained, she asked Dan about his family. His lack of mean things to say about them surprised Françoise. Drama followed money, Dan figured to himself whenever his mother-in-law mentioned any further divergences of similarity. Françoise knew that in Dan's eyes, nobody held higher prominence than his mother, even in death. Instead, she asked in a roundabout way who had the better father, he or Étienne? The question carried only half an expectation of being answered but the response came without hesitation.

"Your husband, for sure."

"You don't want to think about it, at least for a second?"

A host of reasons where his own dad failed but Étienne's succeeded brilliantly never received mention. None of it mattered since he too was dead but had been so for much longer than Françoise's husband. A poor joke offered the only insight into any paternal discontent.

"At least Étienne's dad had more sense than to fight and die in a war for oil a year before he was supposed to retire. Just being a present father is the least of what makes your husband the winner."

"Does Étienne still talk about his dad?" Françoise wondered out loud.

"A healthy amount, according to his therapist."

"How does he speak about him?"

"Very highly."

"Good," she said before offering a warning, "you and I have to make sure it stays that way."

So much with Françoise became lost in translation. An excellent command of English often met betrayal with words or phrases that eluded synonyms in French. For a week until their next Sunday call, Dan contemplated what exactly she meant. Whenever that condition came up in thought, the scant memories he had of Étienne's dad accompanied. A career military man who moved into government contracting after retirement, a seriousness underscored his speech and movement. His thinking also tended to fit the expected mold of such a specimen. But his acceptance of a gay son, especially the only son and last male of the paternal family line, astounded Dan. Stories of negative receptions and attitudes toward that part of Étienne's life pointed that accusatory finger at Françoise. But Dan's own military father never minded a queer son, either. And would an explanation about her remark from the Christmas dinner finally be delivered? The Sunday call finally arrived with many questions in tow.

Dan asked first about her cryptic message last week.

"Étienne always loved him more than me. His dad became a safe place for him when he came out. And to Étienne, that was everything. I had a terrible time with the news. I wanted grandkids. Still do, but now that's on his sister."

That reasoning Dan understood. His mom helped him through his own difficult coming out, not just by being a pillar of love and support, but also because she understood growing up queer, as a lesbian.

"Are you Catholic?" Françoise began, her question confusing to Dan.

"Not practicing. My dad's side of the family is. So...a little?"

"What do you know about the sins of the father?"

"Not much. Why?"

Dan wanted his inquiry to wedge in between those from Françoise but it failed. She continued, unphased. She no longer asked questions but began telling a story.

In the mid-sixties Étienne's dad was attending college

at Tulane University when an accident happened. Fear kept it hidden even from his family, only he and the other boys knew. After years of anguish, the burden of his actions almost succeeded in breaking his mind, so he confessed to Françoise, three months pregnant with her oldest child and only son. Even though the practice of "rolling a queer" fell out of fashion when that Mexican tour guide got killed during the fall of 1958 in the French Quarter, the tradition didn't completely die. On a dare, Étienne's dad and his friends beat a queer kid to death. And they never suffered justice or suspicion. Their crime barely even made the paper. *What's one more dead queer?* the prevailing attitude dared to ponder. Unfortunately for the dead queer.

The revelation knocked all the wind out of Dan's chest. Silence held dominion over the 5G cellular space between him and the surrogate on either end of the phone.

"So, you think that Étienne is gay as punishment for what your husband did?" Dan asked, finally. His other questions stayed in reserve for later. Françoise remained unusually quiet. Dan continued with the same thought, intending to elicit some response to help validate his thinking. "It doesn't mean he's gay because of that—"

"I know that," Françoise abruptly interrupted. No excitement or agitation colored her voice as she continued. Relief seemed to support what she said next. "It means the son had to suffer for the terrible things his father did. Have you never suffered for being gay? Has your life been a picnic? Poor Étienne's sure hasn't."

As her voice trailed off, Dan recalled the stories his husband told him about when he came out, and other incidents that became open wounds only recently beginning to scar. Her confession brought more perplexity. Étienne always said that his mom reacted the worst and that his dad seemed unbothered and only concerned about his son being happy. Dan feared voicing any difference against the opinion Françoise presented. Étienne loved his dad with every ounce of available consideration and for all Dan knew, the reverse was also true of father to son. All this, when added to Françoise's fondness for exaggeration, made the acknowledgment unreliable. Rewriting the narrative to give her better casting and lighting seemed in character. More than likely, she believed the confession of her knowledge about a hate crime to a gay man brought extra forgiveness. Understanding one thing became of paramount importance to Dan.

"Françoise, why are you telling me this?" With that, Dan believed a glimmer of truth might break through a crack in her story. Disappointment would remain. He would detect nothing.

"The same reason my husband told me. To lessen the weight I carried for years. You'll never know what it's like to have to keep a secret like that from a child. Since you all can't have your own kids, I mean."

Dan disregarded the ignorance of his mother-in-law's last statement. From nowhere, he remembered what she said during a prior call. *You and I have to make sure it stays that way.* The ominous words that closed that call rang through his head, deafening him. *You and I...* Françoise settled well into her seventies, but eventually the burden would fall solely on Dan. He understood that now. Her words returned again. And each word produced a miniscule crack in the picture-perfect ideal framed on an imaginary shelf. With her last utterance, Françoise shattered the image of a man Étienne held in the highest esteem. Further proof that nobody owned perfection and the desire to maintain the false veneer of something nonexistent knew no limit.

After the call, Dan thought about his own family, their home built in the mid-nineteen-seventies. The weak structure holding the family unit together never had a chance to survive even a handful of storms. Confidences reveled piecemeal from both parents left the children poisoned from the asbestos-like lies insulating the house The sins of his own father surely sent him to the hell of his own believing, his personal inferno of deceit, unkept promises and selfishness. Dan and his brother vowed never to lie to each other, if not to anybody, ever again. Family as he knew it meant little, but family as he created it meant the world to him. Family was supposed to foster love, comfort and nurturing. Mendacity, affairs and stolen money ruined so much for Dan's family to the point where the realization and knowledge that he now held a secret capable of destroying another's house and reputation took a while to detonate inside his head. Love was often enough to start wars but hate-fueled silence destroyed nations.

Dan saw more of Étienne's dad in him since the infection from Françoise's news took effect. Similar builds, height, even the same red tint to their hair. Their demeanors shared a common calm, and Dan never imagined any violence alive inside his husband. Situations where a less tempered person might punch a wall or face presented no challenge to Étienne's patience. Often just hearing what happened to his husband was enough to send Dan into a rage. Still in the dark as to what he overheard Françoise acknowledge, Dan gleaned enough to determine a reference to some former aggressive action from her husband. This was confusing since no story circulated about anybody getting the upper hand over Françoise. She never confirmed it and he had no idea how to ask with tact. But now Dan began to wonder what exactly lurked inside a heart that he knew to be good. Only hours before, Dan thought the same of Étienne's dad, the man who gifted his son with many other amazing attributes as well. Two of those traits for which Dan felt most grateful for were his husband's patience and forgiveness. In life, Étienne's father must have attempted to gain absolution for a sin guaranteed to earn him a place in hell through living amends with his own gay son. Besides, he knew how Catholics worked: sinners, assholes, and sometimes even murderers during the week, but free of sin and right with God after confession and a couple of Hail Mary's. Whatever the reason, Étienne benefitted greatly from paternal doting. A tinge of jealousy sparked from the friction between that fact and Dan's retentions of his own absent father. The internal grappling concluded with a thought: who exactly was Étienne's dad? Then, abruptly, another: who exactly was Étienne? A brief swell of pride formed when Dan failed to link any of his husband's traits with those of Françoise. One unreliable voice already made for far too many.

"How devoted to telling the truth is your mom?" Dan asked two days after his call with Françoise, once the weight of that agony became too much a burden to bear.

"Depends on who it makes look better in the end."

"Meaning…?"

"She'll tell you anything if it paints a better picture of her," Étienne clarified. "Why do you ask?"

Dan blamed the seed of suspicion sprouting inside his husband's mind as the cause for the question closing Étienne's explanation. Silence prompted a repeat of the inquiry.

"What makes you ask this out of the blue? What did Maman tell you now?"

Both questions were asked through gritted teeth and an uncomfortable smile.

Dan danced around the real reason his husband wanted to know. Revealing exactly why carried the destructive power of an atom bomb. Nothing but scarred ruins would remain; nothing stood a chance of staying the same. Dan loved Étienne too much. Annihilation never held much appeal.

But Étienne kept on prodding – never satisfied. So much that Dan wondered about what exactly might happen if he dropped the bomb. The secret of his husband's father became a weapon. And as a brief glimpse at the full terror of its power unfolded in his head, Dan decided to keep it secreted away. Every atom of his own body, already altered and malignant by the fallout of information, demanded he do otherwise. But the beautiful face in motion before Dan's troubled mind meant more than battles, and more than destruction. Besides, he had an entire arsenal of forgotten dates, ruined birthdays, and three-ways, and so many more offenses to use against his husband in combat.

"You know I don't like it when you ignore me!" Étienne exclaimed. "Are you listening?"

Dan watched Étienne's face distort, the gentle features becoming a scowl. And when that question became the final among several Étienne asked while Dan ignored him, a fissure developed and both sides immediately raised defenses to meet the perceived threat. No matter what, he heard his mother-in-law's voice state in his head: *You and I have to make sure it stays that way.* But Étienne never relented, and Dan's defenses became offenses.

A single, barbed remark tended to have the power of halting any argument. A jarring souvenir from the past often shocked both men from their ferocity just enough to set them both back on the road to forgiveness. Once issued, Étienne escalated his own defenses and launched an attack. A rare occurrence but Dan knew how to parry, dodge and counterattack. When that had no effect, he created a quick half-lie to buy time, regroup and think of a better plan.

"She told me something about your dad that I know is bullshit, okay?"

Étienne bought it and after a deep breath, spoke with his usual calmness. "That's all you had to say. You didn't have to be a dick when all I did was ask a question. And certainly don't ever ignore me again."

Dan clenched his mouth shut, tightened his jaw, and nodded.

"So, what did she say?" Étienne asked as an insolent encore.

"She said your dad had the worst reaction to your being gay and that she was always the more accepting of your parents." Dan became flustered at the issuance of another half-truth. The two he told equaled one whole lie, a low tally, but one too many for a man who aspired to remain honorable to the man he loved.

"Yeah, that is bullshit," Étienne agreed and with conspicuous ease he let go of the subject.

Sleep proved difficult for Dan, tormented while awake and in dreams. Étienne laid next to him all night in bed, expectantly oblivious and still satisfied from two rounds of make-up sex.

The specter of a past not too far gone visited Dan, sat with him, talked to him, with no mind paid to wakefulness or sleep. A presence loomed large in the room, a projection from his overstimulated imagination. Screams stayed stifled. Swapped accusations fell on four deaf ears. Resolution arrived late, or did it at all? So many filmy visions doomed to retreat into recesses too deep for recall.

Odd for Étienne to wake up before Dan, who met his early rising husband with a kiss in the kitchen. Coffee made, the counter cleared and cleaned, the tv switched off, it all pleased Dan but Étienne's presence there so soon in the day confounded his sensibilities. The daily routine followed a specific flow, one moved by his own will. Étienne's making the coffee and cleaning freed time for Dan, but those precious minutes were subjugated to another purpose, also not of his design.

"You're up early," Dan noted after a heavy gulp of coffee.

"Yeah," Étienne returned, "you woke me up pretty early."

"Shit. Sorry. Did I kick you again?"

"Not this time. You sure did have a lot to say, though."

"I have a lot on my mind. You could've made me sleep on the couch."

"Oh no. I wanted to hear what you had to say."

Dan took another hefty slug of coffee. The dark liquid tasted more bitter than Étienne's usual extra strong blend. His eyes fell low and dodged Étienne's attempt to lock gazes. No recollection came to even hint at what he might have said in his sleep. Dreams failed to materialize, and he wracked his brain while the caffeine accelerated a heartrate already racing with worry. "Hmm…" Dan responded with feigned indifference. But the distress showed in the nervous motions animating his body – from the slouched, retreating posture to the slight tremble in his hand as he sat the cup of coffee down. Dan woke up in a pool of sweat and foreboding, but now he drowned under an errant tide of guilt. "I can't even imagine what came out of my mouth." That truth received acceptance from them both and one truth led to another in Dan's mind and his apprehension grew threefold. Karma unleashed a curse for harboring an awful secret. Fear kept any more words from escaping. Another sip of acrid coffee ensured their suppression.

After a moment of unnerving silence, Étienne spoke. "Makes sense. You were out of it. I tried talking to you at first, sometimes that works to calm you down. But nothing was stopping that conversation."

"Who was I talking to?" Dan wondered out loud, "a ghost?"

"I believe so."

"Do we need to call an exorcist? We did just move in, but I haven't noticed anything weird."

"No, not a ghost in the house. But you were talking to somebody dead."

"Who? Tell me if you know."

"I think you were talking to my dad. You called his name a couple times. You also said my name and Maman's, told him how we were. Then the conversation got real interesting. And the conversation turned into yelling and blaming."

"What was that all about?" Dan pretended ignorance.

"You tell me."

"Why, when you look like you already know."

"What did you and Maman really talk about the other day? I don't think you told me the whole truth."

"Dreams can be pretty fucking unreal sometimes. Remember the lyrics to that song we love? Dreams are like water, colorless and dangerous."

"Daniel David O'Hara! I'm being serious!"

"François Étienne Duchamp! I know and I'm engaging my defense mechanism!"

Étienne became insistent, his questions nearly demands. And again, Dan dodged with limited capacity, but now with little success. Étienne was winning this round by wearing down an already defeated man. The last thought he possessed had to be that this time the furtiveness of his husband was for a common good.

And what Dan once thought a potential weapon now weighed him down in battle. The confidential information promised horrible consequences regardless of how it dropped. Dan felt pressure swell up behind his eyes until he felt certain they threatened to pop out of his skull. With that new outlet, the secret had another means of escape. Imaginary hands covered his eyes and mouth. Selective hearing waved away the need for ethereal hands to cover his ears. The visualization of him as a proverbial monkey elicited a grin until his husband's face and tense body stood less than an inch from his own. Tight lips kept the smirk from becoming a full-on laugh.

The expression on Étienne's face stayed frozen in annoyance. Dan's visible discomfort grew, indigestion from the acidic coffee burning the parts of his heart unmarred by restlessness and defeat. He could ruin his own life forever by lying and taking a step toward becoming what he hated, a man like his own father, burning in hell for his duplicity. Or he could destroy three lives and a memory by telling the truth. What all did Étienne hear? How well could he bluff? Dan recoiled, realizing how little he knew his husband when that understanding became imperative. Dan needed to decide whether to lie or tell the truth.

A GAY BODY ODE, OR ARDOR

HELLO STRANGER. It's what your paramour and tormentor says every morning when you wake up. And so, it begins. The mirror shows a lie. What that boy in his bedroom sees differs greatly from how you're seen by that insistent bully at home who steals so much with intimate glimpses every day, he who is your longest-lasting lover and opponent. That young man with daddy issues in the next room appreciates a hard body good for a few hours of pleasure, but now just wonders when you'll leave his house. Your lover at home sees a lump of unimpressive, unmalleable clay. Humans can only do so much, and an older model is capable of even fewer remarkable feats. Thanks to this, you've made of your body the perfect screen readily showing anybody willing to look whatever they care to see.

What you see, looking in the oversized bathroom mirror of that evening's trick, is what others first see before their needs get projected. When good posture is observed, squared shoulders greet the eyes. The arms dangling from the sloped corners have definition implying years of exercise and work. Tattoos litter the contours yet add a beauty to the organic geometry. The chest, covered in a carpet of fur, raises with each breath then retains some of the heft once air leaves the lungs. A trim torso betrays the shell's actual age more than the rest as actual abs still show. At first glance, everything seems in place and well-formed. Easy movements make sense when performed by something in working order. Blue eyes and light hair equal currency for some people. More acute inspection shows cracks around the pools of blue, trenches even burrow into a forehead growing larger from a receding hairline. Still currency for some, but for you, who knows? Less elasticity in the skin means fewer bounce-backs from late nights like this. Muscles appear as if a slow deflation began without notice. But still, everything looks fine – *you* look fine. Nobody cares what you think.

Take a moment. Forget about the impatient boy in the other room. He can wait. Now look in the mirror. Look at the carefully maintained screen, blank and naked. Describe what stares back. Don't start fretting about tomorrow's workout or which part of the body flexing in the mirror will suffer improvement after forty-five minutes of weights and fifteen more of cardio. Everyone knows about the abusive relationship the body suffers at the hands of the mind, also called being gay. Even in moments like this, when partly out of your mind and very much still in your body and focused on its physical sensations.

What should be seen is a veritable checklist of what most gay men would hope for. Stock falls past a certain collection of years but the numbers rebound with a body in near fine condition. When swimming in a civilization fixated on youth and newness, demands to taste vitality and energy weigh heavy with hopes to drown. Even after rudimentary lust sinks enough feelings. But you have a part to play, so keep up the good work. A good actor takes general directions well. Shame the director is unscrupulous. He wants you to be what he sees in magazines and on movie screens. Can you think of any other purpose for a gay man's body to serve?

Dressed in trademark jeans and a white t-shirt, you cut an impressive figure. The plainness of the shirt amplifies your usefulness as a blank screen for others. Whatever they need to see can only become more compelling because you return a display of what they want to see in themselves. Selfless in that regard, but self-absorbed with the priorities of a masculine mind. What anyone wants to envision, they'll get: Daddy, Mama's Boy, Otter, Wolf, Older Gay Man, A Good Time – all that, but not quite, and yet so much more. Blank screens easily stain. Better art graces the halls and walls of museum-like homes; don't let a swollen head ruin what many mistake for a masterpiece. Even higher quality white trash litters far filthier floors, good sir. But only you know what you really are, even if you refuse to acknowledge the truth behind your only proper function. Those muscles that bulge in all manner of motion feed on blood. That pales compared to the internal muscles, moving more blood, oxygen, and shit, through organs and tubes like ticking time bombs. All that beauty, that rancor, involuntarily serving a mind that rots you from the inside out, punishing an otherwise superlative body for its age.

Blow the beautiful young man half your age a kiss goodbye and return the promise neither of you will keep about seeing each other again soon. One more glimpse in another mirror by the door. Gay male bodies are currency, their worth defined by solid lines and firm, stable assets. Feel your rise in value as you walk out into the night air and take a deep breath. Oxygen-rich blood flows from the lungs to the heart, along with it, the sensation of existing. Purpose is purpose, even if misguided. Another day comes tomorrow and brings along other chances from a bucket with fewer prospects to grab every time your hand reaches in.

USELESS, USELESS

The news came over social media that Carlton Monroe died. Tragically. Accidentally. But at least while doing something he always wanted to do. Pretty sure he even once joked that he'd been dying to try deep sea diving. The gods answered his prayers in one messy moment. The irony was lost on nobody who knew him. Retirement from the military at forty-five with still so much life ahead of him. A wife. Two kids. They watched from the boat as Carlton went under the shimmering blue water in one piece then came out of the ruddy water in chunks. The memorial service resembled a pharaonic sendoff. Edward Weathers, a civilian co-worker, viewed the sum of Carlton's life as worthy of respect, but not so much adulation. By comparison, Edward wondered what his own might be worth in the end.

Then one day, Edward felt really old. Not falling apart in body or mind, just the understanding that most of what occupied his thinking happened in the past. Time for me to do something about *that*, he thought. The first step came off more as him dipping a toe in a puddle. He first became Eddie but settled on Ed. Plain, old Ed. The few people he encountered only seemed to be happy for the one less syllable of his company. The new abbreviation meant nothing to anybody he met after his great transformation into Ed. The novel confidence manifested at times when the new Ed appealed to people in bars who couldn't see the reality of his age advancing across his face in the form of lines, wrinkles, and gray hair. Deep pockets to intoxicate certainly helped. More drinks than necessary and effusive compliments tended to seal the deal. Then the inevitable morning after filled with expectation turning to disappointment then dismay. A lonely shower washed off the smell and outward evidence but inside Ed felt cold in spite of the scalding water turning his skin beet red.

Summer ended with Ed's more concerted stabs at feeling valuable in another person's life. He needed someone in his life to make him feel important, but nobody needed Ed in their life. The time came when more leaves littered the ground than the branches. A chill had yet to maintain its permanence during the day, but the evenings hinted at what the following weeks might bring. Out for a walk as the sun began its descent in the west, Ed thought about the fact that he had entered the autumn of his life. More beautiful foliage had fallen and been trampled on several times already while he reminisced. He couldn't look at anything without feeling old. Dry, crumbling leaves cracked and shuffled along with his feet. The noise and smell carried him back many years since his love of the season remained constant. But his usual delight gave way to a feeling more forlorn, wistful about days and times gone by like a morose Romantic poet. The neighborhood stood still, cast in the golden sheen of sunset. But it was fool's gold. A bitter gust of wind whipped at him, to remind him of what always nipped at that beauty's heels.

Ed preferred to move about in silence, so he took great care in avoiding the dusting of dead leaves on the sidewalks leading to his apartment. Easier said than done, considering the multitude blanketing the concrete. Motion on a balcony across the street stopped him in his tracks and stole his concern for quietness. A boy dressed only in a white t-shirt and black running shorts watered plants too green for the season. He himself appeared too sensitive for the oncoming cold, and even too green for Ed. A perfect view of the boy illuminated by a gentle and glowing outdoor light had its rewards. Vivacity radiated from his face, his skin, his movements. Too much life had yet to break his skin with troubles or hunch his back and shoulders with burden. A little body hid just under the boy's clothing. Dark hair crowned a head that saw the world through eyes even darker than the oncoming night. Then the boy went inside, and the balcony light went out. Ed followed suit, opening his front door to enter but never turning off his porch light.

Anytime Ed went outside for any reason, his casual regard drifted in the direction of the boy's apartment and balcony. The blinds stayed closed day and night. No sign of life showed for an insufferable duration. Ed joked to himself that he must've seen a ghost but then one night, lights peeked through half-opened Venetian blinds. He took it to mean that the boy had returned from the dead, a sign of spring in the chill of a fall evening.

From this intimate vigil, Ed hoped to see some other sign of life coming from within the apartment across the street. Nothing happening on either side afforded Ed time to ponder why he obsessed so much over a boy he had only barely seen once. Curious desires conjured many things for this starved imagination: How old was the boy? Who was he? Why the compulsion to know? Other examinations about personality types, what his voice sounded like, experiences so far, his sexuality, so much possessed his head to keep his gaze fixed on the lit apartment across the street. An answer or two promised to reveal themselves at some point.

"See something interesting over there?" a detached voice asked. The accusatory tone held a hint of sarcasm, but to the startled Ed it translated into irritation.

Quick glimpses right and left detected no one. Sweeping looks slowed down the more confused Ed became. Until the voice spoke again.

"Over here," it said, calling Ed's attention at last to the source. In the dark, the boy stepped from his expert concealment among the shadows of the trees. "Is there a reason you're spying on my house?"

"What makes you think I'm spying? I'm standing in the open. You're the one hiding in the dark watching me. See something interesting yourself?" Ed's attempted swagger cracked along with his voice. Nerves took full responsibility for the uncharacteristic behavior. The boy offered an apology.

"I've noticed you around the neighborhood," the boy continued as he approached Ed's balcony. More of him came into better view.

"I can't say the same about you," Ed returned. He instantly regretted the comment. Now proof existed of his espionage. That the boy took notice of, along with Ed's mortification.

"Noted," was all the boy said in return. Following an unbearable silence, he offered his name. "I'm Noah."

"I'm Ed. Pleased to meet you."

"Finally, huh?" A coy smile formed on his face as he teased the older man. "So, are you gonna come down and talk to me or just stay up there? Don't be scared. I only bite if I feel threatened. And you don't scare me so come on down."

Ed smiled, not really knowing why. His apprehension came from fear of that unknown motive, not from a fear of violence.

The kid, Noah, presented a slighter build than Ed's. The young physique appeared better suited for offering fantasies instead of pain. Once outside, Ed approached Noah, the diminishing space between them awful with energy. A sense of completion came from nowhere.

Noah extended his hand as a further greeting. "You're even more handsome up close." He delivered the sentence with Ed's hand still in his.

Ed blushed like a schoolboy and thanked Noah for the compliment with a stuttered acceptance. The chill in the air was an excuse for the stammer and shaky hands. Noah only smiled back.

Small talk went back and forth but within that limited expanse of time, both learned quite a bit about the other. And the back and forth ended with the expectation that both would learn quite a bit from the other.

"It's time I get back inside. My window is that one," Noah said, pointing to the window directly across from Ed's "I'll wave goodnight before I go to bed."

"Okay," Ed said, not knowing a better response. "It was nice to meet you," he then said, offering his hand to shake again.

Noah looked down at the goodbye gesture presented then back into the face of its owner. "I'd really rather kiss you, instead."

The statement's deliverance came so matter of fact that it took Ed off guard. Noah's face moved in and stopped Ed's lips before they could protest. The taste of respective suppers mingled on their tongues while their mouths moved in uncanny unison. A stupid look remained on Ed's face after Noah pulled away. The boy smiled and delivered a final peck on the older man's lips.

"Talk to you later," Noah said over his shoulder before licking his lips. He had already began walking the few yards home.

Ed cursed himself for not getting Noah's number and almost asked but glaring at the boy's ass while he walked away hypnotized him into thinking about other things. Like staring at the window directly across from his anytime it was dark outside, and lights indicated Noah was home, for instance.

For a week Ed saw no sign of Noah. During the day, all the blinds in the windows remained closed and at night no lights signaled an empty house. Which to Ed meant no contact. And since no new information about the boy flowed in, he had to fill in the blanks himself. Whatever he asked himself needed answers from Noah in order to be truly understood. Lacking that knowledge meant little as Ed tried anyway. But only a more incomplete picture formed from what their introduction intended and where their friendship might go next, if anywhere. Ed stopped and realized he was getting ahead of himself. He always did. Instead, his concentration turned to next time not forgetting to ask Noah for his number.

While staring in the mirror Ed asked himself why Noah found him handsome. Nothing exemplary. Not even anything worthwhile that he himself as a gay man would grant a doubletake. An assortment of skin care containers dotted the sink, and he thanked them for living up to their claims. Regardless, he believed everything about himself could improve. With better exercise, more sleep, and all the other self-preservation routines men his age undertook to regain vitality, Ed knew the possibilities of transformation. Every morning before breakfast he began to bend, pull, and mold his body into something more formidable. Blood flowed again with the quick circulation of youth. Soon he might see what Noah did: some handsome man more than twice his age who was worth kissing.

Then one night, as Ed finished his nightly constitutional and last bout of cardio for the day, a whistle brought the attention he focused on breathing towards the apartment across the street. Noah's light was on, and the window open. He leaned out of the frame, beautifully backlit and glowing in the middle of the windowsill. He appeared dramatic and spectacular clad only in his underwear. He motioned Ed closer, his finger extended over his lips.

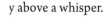 y above a whisper.

 l as an explanation. "Can't
in a mood. Give me your
gits of his phone number
equest for silence. After a
urned to walk back to his

apartment. Before stepping inside, he turned to look again in the direction of his neighbor's window. To his surprise, Noah still stood bordered in the soft glow of his bedroom light. His gaze remained locked on Ed, who could only quickly walk inside and lock the door. *How stupid to be scared of an eighteen-year-old boy,* he thought to himself right before his phone buzzed its notice that a message arrived.

What was the best part of your day? The message read.

Ed took a moment to reply, careful not to assume an excessive familiarity. *It's been a shitty day, so I'll say talking to you has been the best part so far.*

Heart emojis responded to Ed's sappy text. That opened the

flood gates for more intimacy to develop. As the conversation veered towards a more delicate nature, Ed began his tests on the boy's limits. He wanted Noah. He understood that now. But he still had no idea why he found a child so compelling. "Stoopid childrens" Ed called Noah and his useless generation at one point, the deliberate misspelling for emphasis. Then came a series of pics, one after the other, a slow striptease out of his underwear that showed off the contours and lines of a body with still so much to learn about itself. For instance, the shots displayed how well Noah's body looked, but the boy had no idea the authority it commanded. Taut flesh held fast to muscles under construction. Hairless from the waist up, his legs and ass blanketed with dark fur. And when the last picture came through, Ed's eyes bulged at seeing one of the most perfect cocks he'd ever seen. Ed followed suit and sent his own sequence of shots. He delighted that Noah found an older body attractive, let alone worthy of praise. Esteem grew as Ed congratulated himself on the workouts and felt his uselessness slacken. Both saved the series of pics for later, and for inspiration.

So close though so far, the rest of Noah's first semester had to be spent learning remotely from home. All Noah disclosed at first reeked of untruths and new explanations fell through gaping holes in a poorly maintained lie. After only a week of near constant messaging, Ed knew to expect he'd be left in the dark about many things in the boy's life. Despite living yards apart and an urgent insistence about how Ed rose to a place of prominence thanks to a combination of brains, handsomeness and compassion, any other outward displays from the boy had yet to manifest. Ed fast realized his fate of giving more to their friendship than the boy ever would. But the precociousness of youth helped Noah get away with so much. Well-timed messages and sexts kept the hook dangerous and firm in Ed's cheek.

As Noah began to act out, much to Ed's astonishment, so did Ed, much to both their bewilderment. Both needed attention and the other sufficed, proximity playing the bigger part. The boy's dad stayed away with work while his mom stayed home but in a haze of pills with vodka, all unpleasant. And working the rest of the school year from home meant long hours alone, trapped inside and neglected. Ed related to the feeling of isolation. Though his stemmed from self-seclusion, the effect of loneliness reminded Ed to disparage his own while speculating how it should play out for Noah. So much life ahead of the boy and so much behind the older man. Little shared experience was unimportant. Many other commonalities and interests made for much to discuss and allowed a comprehension to develop and deepen the friendship between the disparate neighbors. Both benefitted from conversations about their views on life and growing up gay in different generations. Noah finally had an adult to talk to and Ed finally had someone who acted interested in what he had to say. They found in one another exactly what each of them needed at the time. Ed just needed to keep his expectations low after placing Noah on so high a pedestal.

Personal information was coaxed in a way Ed employed before, even if that intention never existed. But the method worked. He got upset when the boy refused to see him in person, choosing instead to deflect with an insipid meme. Ed already detested the meaningless existence of memes, especially when the joke ended up on him. Another reason to loathe the internet and its bastard offspring social media. Flippant responses infuriated Ed further until a meltdown occurred, complete with all the trappings of self-righteous indignation. *Stoopid childrens,* Ed ended those arguments thinking. And the boy ended up reduced to what resembled a whelping spaniel, head low with remorse and eyes full of desperate forgiveness. But then all these passions came flooding back to a lesser degree on a lower tide with Noah's refusal to make up in person, a kiss the bare minimum asked. To keep the delicate balance, Ed maintained his push at a minimum to keep Noah in his infectious good spirits. And all the reservations the boy's excuses promoted remained locked away for another time.

Late one night Noah messaged Ed, the lead-in picture of him half-naked. Expecting another round of hot pictures and empty promises, he jumped up when instead a request came over to meet Noah outside. *Put on clothes, it's almost winter,* Ed texted. Within minutes, both of them stood outside under naked tree branches and the harsh glow of a bare overhead streetlight.

"You're not afraid your family might see?" Ed asked.

"They're not home. First time both are gone at the same time in months."

"Then why are we standing outside?" Ed asked with an impish grin.

"Because we have cameras. That's why I have bags of trash. I'm not allowed out otherwise. I only have a few minutes."

"Then let's go inside my house. The owner won't care." Ed felt his attempts to seduce were becoming useless.

"Walk with me to the dumpster?" Noah said, a single eyebrow raised. Ed found that affectation irresistible, so he complied with what the boy asked.

Trash discarded, Noah grabbed Ed's hand and hurried them

both behind the dumpster. A slash of darkness concealed them from the waist down. The boy smiled at his older friend before placing both hands on Ed's shoulders to push him down to his knees. Shrouded in darkness, Ed freed the boy's dick with expert precision. Never had the appeal and the fervor combined to such astounding effect than when Ed sucked Noah off, as if communicable beauty and youthfulness existed in the boy's uncurdled seed. Within five minutes Ed got his wish and waited the rest of the night until early morning wide awake for proof positive he had been restored.

The expectation of more physical contact withered along with the properties of Noah's fresh sap. Flimsy excuses piled mile high but blew away with ease. Ed's previous method of maintaining dialogue fared little. Light slipped from his sky. Energy faded to a melodramatic degree as the older man suffered from the consequences of an abrupt exclusion barring him from confidences and the source of his recent exhilaration. Affected, Ed promised himself that anything must be done to stay in the boy's good graces, in the light of a sun with well over seven million more years than he had left to burn. If only Ed knew the satisfaction of that need reciprocated. No proof still materialized thus far.

Thanksgiving loomed a day away and a bitterness sparked in the gray air of November. Winter nipped at the autumn splendor enough to make Ed stay inside most days. Noah used the excuse as well, but only to echo his older friend's reasons for hibernation. The boy's family left their son alone and to his own devices inside the prison of surveillance, mood stabilizers, and neglect. But his friend kept him company through texts, happy to help and distract despite Noah's unusually heavy and somber disposition. A threat of impending hostility. Ed was scared enough to mention his discomfort. Noah's tones and language shifted and turned a sharp right. A new erratic pattern directed the boy's responses.

Intense jabs at Noah's parents bruised the conversation until Ed signed off. He understood the boy's frustration but tried to remind Noah that he still lived under his parents' roof and paid zero dollars in rent. Did that give them the right to incarcerate their son? No. And if he really felt like a prisoner, he could always run away. *Or,* Noah texted, *they could just fucking die already.*

An onslaught of texts first thing in the morning had become commonplace so Ed smiled at seeing all the messages from Noah. Thinking the boy slept off whatever was bothering him the night before, the reality of rage burning from the blue message bubbles confirmed the opposite. Fury-filled sentences waited to be read and expected sympathetic replies. A question followed every vile accusation from the boy. *Can you believe they treat me like this?* When he repeated his parents' request that he stay home for Thanksgiving. *Why bother having a kid at all?* Noah asked after admitting his parents detested having a gay son. So much already to deal with before the sleep was wiped from Ed's already tired eyes.

Retorts came as the caffeine infiltrated his blood and brain. Easier to think at last, Ed noted a marked difference in the quality of Noah's messages. The boy had been upset at his parents before, but the flagrant frenzy of menace caused concern. Once Ed declared his worry, Noah switched gears and back-pedaled. *I'm only kidding,* he promised. *I'm just angry because I'm tired of being a prisoner in my own home,* he assured.

And Ed accepted it as long as Noah kept his promise to redirect that negative energy into something productive.

An hour plus later saw the completion of Noah's one-hundred and eighty-degree turnabout. Delight filled the effervescent blue bubbles instead of the previous indignation. When asked what changed his mind, Noah replied with a cagey wisecrack about finally leveling out without help from his medication. The boy always had difficulty convincing his older friend since Ed new the games of an eighteen-year-old boy starved for attention. Noah won in the end by asking for a ride to his aunt and uncle's house a half-hour away in Great Falls.

The assurance of proximity to the boy at last, his literal fountain of youth, knocked reason from Ed's thought processes. Sweet words and even sweeter promises swept enough concern away for him to cave in to the boy's request for a ride. Any harm done wouldn't be on him, Ed concluded at the thought of Noah starting a food fight during turkey dinner. What a laugh.

In person, Ed detected a different hazard lurking beneath the surface of Noah's demeanor from earlier. His hands shook a bit whenever he talked, and an impediment chopped up the fluidity of any sentences he spoke.

"I'm just nervous. I owe you for the ride." Noah said, placing his jittery hand on Ed's upper thigh. "I've never done this before," the boy admitted as he undid Ed's belt, zipper, and fly.

Another fib, Ed thought as the boy expertly withdrew his dick and eventually his substance.

The few minutes between finishing and reaching their destination among the mansions of Great Falls were filled with conversations about Thanksgiving plans. Ed had none and intended to keep it that way, when Noah asked if he wanted to join him. How awkward to show up unannounced as a complete stranger.

"I could tell them you're coming. They've been blowing up my phone since we left." Noah meant what he said about the extended invitation.

"Why are they doing that?" Ed asked.

"They're probably worried when I'll show up. *If* I show up."

"You told them you were on the way, right?"

"Kinda."

The two syllables floated on an air of eerie distrust. Ed rolled the window down to clear the atmosphere but that only made the space in the car colder. *One minute away,* Ed noted to himself after a glimpse at the phone's GPS.

Parked one house down, after keeping the man suspended in an insufferable silence, Noah thanked Ed for the lift. The boy's goodbye sounded more like a farewell than a "see you later." Ed agreed to a hug outside of the car with a reluctant tear nearly escaping his eye. Their heights matched so the embrace felt to both like a perfect fit. Something hard poked into Ed's belly during the tightest part of the embrace. An alarmed look at Noah's waist provoked him to blame a belt buckle and apologize. Noah said he hated his family's dedication to dressing for dinner. Then the stutter returned, and the trembling took over his hands again.

"Well," Noah began, "one more kiss goodbye?" Without waiting for permission, he grabbed Ed's face and kissed him long and deep. Care was taken to keep their waists from meeting. "See?" Noah said, "you're not useless like you think. You've truly made my day. Twice."

The boy smiled demurely, and Ed blushed.

"You're not useless either, even if you're *Stoopid Childrens*," Ed reminded Noah. "Go. I'll see you later."

"More than likely," Noah replied without hesitation.

Ed watched the boy walk to the gate at the beginning of the house's long driveway, type a code or speak into a box, then enter the gates opened and closed to swallow him up into a world he truly hated. Forlorn, Ed got in his car and drove home, his head filled with all the matters collected since knowing Noah, their subsequent concerns and wistful regret, and dismissed any forthcoming resolutions as insubstantial without input from Noah. *An early bedtime for sure,* Ed determined.

Unsure of the compulsion, Ed woke up the next day to watch the news. The Black Friday Wal-Mart fights always entertained, this he knew and looked forward to seeing. But the local news only reported on a murder-suicide in an affluent neighborhood in Northern Virginia. Ed recognized the neighborhood and one of the faces flashing across the screen in sickening HD. Ed's breakfast cereal went soggy as he got his terrible fill of the morning news.

A knock on his door led to an interview with the police that cleared Ed of any knowledge or involvement of the crime. And at the end of the examination, he felt glad his possible fifteen minutes of fame got cut in half by not being more than an unwitting driver in *the* crime of the holiday season. Ed still had seven and a half minutes left and who knows how many useful years ahead to ruin however he deemed acceptable. Though he would always be grateful to Noah and the juvenile infatuation that developed, doomed to not last long but certain to provide an aftershock lasting for years. And Ed never stopped thinking of all the promise squandered to make Noah so tremendously useless within six loud and quick flashes of light.

Jarrod Campbell is a writer living in the Northern Virginia suburbs of Washington, DC. His fictions, essays, reviews and poetry have appeared online and in print with *Northwest Review*, *Boner World* (Berlin), *Heavy Feather Review, Roi Faineant Press*, and others.

ACKNOWLEDGMENTS

First and foremost, eternal gratitude and millions of thanks to Eric David Roman and Adam Prestegord, two of the best fellow scribes I am grateful to call friends and members of the Enclave. You both have spent so much time and energy with these fictions, offering amazing feedback and guidance that this simple note seems insufficient. Here's to many more years of laughs and literature.

Next, I'd like to thank the people who graciously humored me enough to provide feedback, inspiration, or both, in no particular order: Elise Roell, Cassondra Thomas, Bryant Ariza-Vizcaino, Nikki Drag-Kposowa, Kris Smet, Cory Firestine, Daniel P. Miller, Jessica Clay, Eric Melton, Joseph Rough, Edward P. Jones, Danny McCaslin, my close and treasured family, and any others I surely forgot. Your eyeballs and importance to my life and work are forever valued. Also in this category, I'd like to thank Kellie Scott-Reid, Tiffany M. Storrs and the other editors of Roi Fainéant Press for being early believers in my work. I've gushed enough already, though here is yet another gigantic, heartfelt THANK YOU!

Je dois également remercier Juliette Dubois d'avoir emmené Chris et moi au Studio 1928 lors de la plus fantastique tournée cinématographique de Paris, où le plus grand photomaton au monde existe et crée des photos étonnantes pour les couvertures de livres.

Finally, it is necessary to thank James Reich and Stalking Horse Press for the immense honor and privilege of being a part of this most wonderful literary family. Good sir, it has been such an unbelievable experience working with you, a writer I consider one of the best and most brilliant working today. Thank you for your time, editorial expertise, and patience with me and my technological deficiencies. I don't encounter "dream come true" moments often, so the fact that I'm now a part of the Stalking Horse stable with so many other writers I admire and respect still feels like a fantasy.